HUSTLIN' fo' LOVE

Brothaz 4 Lyfe

COREY N. SMALLS

HUSTLIN' FO' LOVE
BROTHAZ 4 LYFE

iUniverse books may be ordered through booksellers or by contacting:

iUniverse
1663 Liberty Drive
Bloomington, IN 47403
www.iuniverse.com
1-800-Authors (1-800-288-4677)

ISBN: 978-1-5320-4468-7 (sc)
ISBN: 978-1-5320-4467-0 (e)

Library of Congress Control Number: 2019904993

Print information available on the last page.

iUniverse rev. date: 04/29/2019

CHAPTER 1

"**C**OREY, GET UP, AND CLEAN THAT room! It's already after eleven thirty, and you're still in bed!" Corey's mother yelled.

She was the mother of four boys, all from the man she'd vowed to spend the rest of her life with. She always had wanted a daughter, but she'd given up after their fourth try. Although she never had experienced what it was like to have a little girl around, she loved the feeling of being the only queen on the board, surrounded by the strong men within her household.

Her hardworking husband, Dennis, was her king. Their two older sons, Teflon and C.O were the knights, and their two baby boys, Grouch and Redeyes, were the rooks. She felt protected!

Gayle disliked that her four boys had dropped out of school and not furthered their educations to become successful in life. Instead, they all had become victims of the streets. Regardless, whether her boys grew up with or without high school diplomas or college degrees, she would always love her boys.

"All right, Mama!" C.O responded with his eyes closed, and then he rolled over to get more rest. "Damn Mama, man," he mumbled.

"And stop cussing in this darn house!" his mother yelled.

"I didn't say a cuss word, Mama," he lied. He smiled under the thick blankets he'd missed so much. He then rolled over and lay flat on his back to regain awareness of where he was. *Damn, I can't believe I'm home again.*

The thought echoed in his mind.

Damn! I'm here lying in my mothafucking bed! He smiled. *What the fuck?*

His heart throbbed at a fast pace with great excitement.

C.O noticed the old penitentiary smell, which usually mixed with the scent of commissary cleaning materials, no longer existed. He heard no clashing sounds of the brass skeleton keys that was always carried by correctional officers, the sound that'll antagonized the prisoners' minds. There were no officials yelling to announce nine o'clock movements or cafeteria shift changes.

He heard no sounds of metal scraping against slick concrete walls and floors around him as dangerous prisoners sharpened their penitentiary knives. For the first time in years, he was at peace.

He just layed in bed—not because he was tired but to be sure it really was his lovely mother's voice he'd heard in his sleep.

"Corey!" his mother yelled from the living room for the second time.

Damn, I'm really home. Corey smiled to himself.

He inhaled and then exhaled air from his lungs with his eyes now open. He thought about his life and where he should begin.

In May 2001, he got caught up in a drug bust with his boys and took all the blame. He felt it wouldn't be fair to see his crew do time, when he was already on the run from probation violations.

"Fuck that. All that dope belongs to me. Y'all can let my homeboys go," he told the arresting officer, who was over the SLED unit. At the time, he did not know the girl he loved so much would later betray him. She was his world, and not long before he went to jail in Horry County, she gave birth to their first son, Tahshawn.

C.O and Cristal met February 1st, 1997, at the Inlet Square Mall. She was only fourteen, and C.O was sixteen. Before then, he'd been in the hood, pushing crack for a local drug dealer.

He wanted to be like his supplier because everyone looked up to him, but sadly, his supplier got killed by a Georgetown County cop.

Dirty had taken care of his business and run the hood with ease. The nigga had been so flossy that he'd given the letter *f* to the word *flossin'*.

Every Sunday, he would visit Dirty's grave site by himself to smoke a blunt and put him down on the bullshit going on in the hood. Although Dirty was dead and gone, C.O felt he was the only gangsta he could talk to.

"A lot of shit has changed since you left, Dirty. Them out-of-town niggas coming around thinking all is sweet.

But you know it's not going down!

Them niggas isn't pushing none of their work on the Hot Road. And like Jojo and Earl would say, 'They'll either smoke it or trick it.

'Cause they're not selling shit on our block. I'm going to hold the fort down my nigga. I promise!

I mean like…, I'm not big-time yet. But with the few grams I'm flipping, I'll do the best I can to keep the feins satisfied and keep them duck-ass niggas off our block."

C.O then took his last pull of the blunt, and laid the other half on the ground on top of Dirty's grave, then walked away.

"Love you, my nigga!"

Right after the death of his role model, He began to live his life without giving a fuck.

He later left home and found comfort in selling drugs, smoking weed, fighting, robbing out-of-town dope dealers, and making them pack their shit and move to another town.

He was living a double life, being in love with Cristal, and the streets.

And to his surprise, he'd learn that she has never been involved with a true thug before, until she'd met him.

She wanted to show him there was a lot more in life than being a street runner and getting into trouble.

To calm him down, she later gave him his first piece of pussy, not knowing it would only make him worst.

Afterward, he shot at every nigga who laid eyes on her.

"Corey, I said get up and clean this room, boy."

His mother was in the bedroom doorway, and before he had the opportunity to quickly hop out of his comfortable bed he slept in, she yanked the blanket from around his head.

He lightly wiped the cold from his eyes, then noticed his mother standing over him, with her arms folded across her chest mean mugging him, She'd caught him still lying in bed!

He smiled.

"Corey don't you play with me!

You need to get up and clean this room.

And I'm not going to keep repeating myself either," she said angrily.

"Mama, I'm getting up, man.

It's just that I'm tired," C.O said while remaining in bed.

"Tired of doing what? Don't think you're going to make this a habit, sleeping all day, Corey.

Before you came home, this room stayed clean."

He was tired of hearing his mother fussing so he got up and began cleaning his room.

Hi later heard loud music coming from outside.

He peeked out the window and noticed his father out in the yard working on his truck.

He laughed at the sight and shook his head.

"Some things just don't ever change. Welcome back C.O This is home sweet home baby,"

he said to himself cheerfully.

Seconds later, he saw an all-gray 750Li BMW with twenty-two-inch deep-dish chrome rims pulling into their driveway and eased up to his father.

He wanted to know who his daddy was talking to.

Moments later, he saw his father point toward the house, and the unknown occupant stepped out of the car.

The sight caught him by surprise.

Damn, that's Tef? he thought excitingly.

He hurried outside to hug his brother after many years of not seeing him.

He respected that his brother Teflon held him down when no one else seemed to care.

Without Teflon, he wouldn't have had any food or hygiene in his locker.

"Eh boy, it's good to see you home my nigga. I didn't know you was home until Pops called me." Teflon smiled.

He'd missed his little brother.

"Yeah, I came home yesterday."

C.O paused to get a good look at his brother's BMW.

"Dang my nigga, this 750 is off the chain! How much you spend on it?"

Teflon looked at his daddy and then back at his little brother.

"Put it like this bro...All knowledge isn't good knowledge.

Do you want to go for a ride?"

Teflon asked his brother while looking at him and notice Corey has gain a lot of weight.

"Hell yeah, but I want you to know that I'm on house arrest my nigga, and I need to be back at the house before three o'clock."

Teflon shook his head in disagreement with the law.

Ever since his brother was young, the system always had had a way of keeping C.O trapped.

"Damn, they got you on house arrest?

I thought you were done with that shit bra. The system got you all fucked up man.

Fuck it, Let's go for a ride. I'll have you back by then."

C.O noticed how his brother's swag had advanced over the years.

He wore a True Religion outfit with Mauri gator loafers.

C.O had butterflies in his stomach at the thought of getting back into the game and getting his money right.

He knew it would take some time before he saw the type of money Teflon was touching, but when his time came, his plan was to have more money than his big brother Tef, not out of jealousy, but to know there was a challenge.

It'd help him stay focused.

While driving around town he couldn't believe how much Horry County had grown.

His brother took him to places that were newly developed and took him to places that were still under construction.

From Murrells Inlet to North Myrtle Beach, it all felt new to him.

But there was something missing.

There were people he missed and wanted to see badly: his son and the mother of his child.

He glanced at his brother, and right away, he wanted Teflon to take him to his baby mother's house, being they were already near the Burgess community.

"Yo Teflon, when was the last time you saw my baby mama punk ass?"

He asked suspiciously, trying his best not to sound too concerned.

"Man, I'm going to be honest with you.

I barely be around! So I can't tell you the last time I saw her,"

Teflon spoke with a slow but strong tone. He have a strong deep voice that ran in the family.

"I'm going to be real with you: that bitch isn't shit, man.

Cause when I went to prison, she played me to the highest degree."

C.O paused.

Memories of Cristal doing him wrong flashed in his mind. The thoughts made his nostrils flared.

He felt she deserved a closed-hand slap to the face.

Teflon shook his head.

"Well, why you want to see her if you feel she played you fucked-up?"

The question hit C.O by surprise. "Teflon I don't want to see her, I want to see my lil man.

So I don't know what the fuck you're talking about."

He felt guilty for lying.

He knew he wanted to see his son's mother as well, even though she'd turned her back on him to fuck with someone else.

That bitch! How could she do that to me? He thought confusingly.

He tried to count the ways of why and how she would have him so fucked-up over her.

From 1997 to 2005, C.O's heart, mind, body, and soul had craved only the mother of his child.

He cared for no one else!

Teflon drove down memory lane and eased into Cristal's mother's driveway.

The anger C.O had felt on the inside toward his son's mother turned into a feeling of nervousness.

He blushed when he felt his brother glance toward him.

That ho has my head fucked up badly. I have to find a way to shake this bitch, man.

"Damn nigga, why you blushing so hard?" Teflon notice his brother smiling to himself.

"Fuck you nigga. I'm not blushing. It's the sun beaming in my face.

You forget it's the month of May."

He tried his best to convince his big brother with a good lie, but he knew Teflon wasn't buying it.

"Nigga, shut up! I don't see any sun beaming in my ride fool.

You know damn well you're still feeling Cristal.

And I'll bet you anything, if she wanted to get married, your dumb ass would build an altar in her yard."

Teflon twisted his mouth and waited for another one of his brother's in-denial responses.

"Teflon, you're tripping for real now. I'm not marrying that bitch after she did that bullshit to me while I was away for those five years." They laughed together.

I can't believe my own brother tried to play me just now.

He was upset that his brother had saw him of being weak over Cristal. And the sad thing is, he knew he were weak.

When they entered her mother's yard, right away, he saw his lover, his enemy, the creator of his love life, the woman he felt he could have trusted with his heart—if she hadn't neglected him.

She shared a life with him, their son's life, but it meant nothing to her.

She was standing next to her Benz, looking beautiful. Her smooth round face was coated with a caramel-brown complexion.

Deep dimples appeared whenever she smiled and showed the even white teeth he loved so much.

She looked beautiful in her tight Baby Phat jeans and a pink halter top with *Diva* written across the chest.

She was a size ten in the waist, with a flat stomach.

Her full lips looked sweet and tasty with pink lip gloss applied.

His dick began to stand at attention, until his brother interrupted his thoughts of fucking her with hatred and desperate need.

"Damn, nigga, go see your Addams family, and stop daydreaming about that pussy."

They both laughed for the second time.

"Fuck you, Teflon!"

He got out of the car and walked toward Cristal's mother, and gave her a hug.

"Hi, Corey, it's good to see you again.

Are you going to stay out of trouble this time? 'Cause you know your son needs you.

Cristal can't raise him by herself," Mrs. Karen said.

"Yes, ma'am, I'm going to stay out of trouble. Cause I don't want to go back to prison."

The thought of him going back to prison made him shivered on the inside.

"You want to see how much he's grown?"

C.O became light-headed, and his hands began to sweat.

He was nervous!

"Yes, ma'am, that's why I'm here. I miss him so much."

Mrs. Karen called for his son Tahshawn, to come see his father. It hurt him when his own son didn't know him.

C.O reached out for him, but Tahshawn kept pulling away. His daddy was a stranger to him. All he could do was stare at his son with hurt in his eyes.

He felt Cristal could have avoided what was happening between them at the moment, bringing Tahshawn to visit him while he was away.

He kissed his son on the forehead.

"I'm sorry for not being here, son. I love you, okay? I'll make it up to you. I promise."

He then gave Cristal a last look before walking toward his brother teflon car, and noticed her staring at him.

She had a lustful look in her eyes that he refused to acknowledge.

His face contorted from the anger he felt. Without speaking, he kept walking.

Stupid bitch!

After he hopped back into the 750Li BMW, the thought of his son not knowing who he was bothered him.

"Damn, Teflon, I'm hurt as fuck, yo. My own fucking son don't even know who the fuck I am.

And I blame my stupid-ass baby mother for that shit, bra."

C.O wanted to scream but maintained his composure.

He wiped his face with both hands in frustration and leaned back into his seat.

"Lil' dawg, hear me out. I know it hurts.

But on some real shit, you can't put all the blame on Cristal. She really didn't leave you.

You left her and my nephew out here by themselves when you went to prison.

You chose that life!" Teflon said.

"You can't blame nobody for all that hot-boy shit you been on back then and later went to prison for.

And now you want a bitch to wait on you? If you wanted the family life, you should've left the game alone.

So it's all your fault if your son doesn't recognize his father."

Teflon reached over and tapped his brother on the shoulder to cheer him up.

"All I can tell you bra bra, is pick up on the lost time, and build a bond with him that's not there. Don't worry about Cristal right now.

It's like this: if you beat a bitch pussy with a belt, she leaves and then comes back.

Trust me. She belongs to you.

In other words, if it's meant to be with you and her, you'll get your family back."

C.O kept his eyes ahead of him.

"So as of right now, just be a good father to your child, 'cause he's innocent my nigga."

As mad as he was, C.O knew Teflon was right. Without saying a word, he just sat there and thought about being there for his son cause he hadn't been there for him in the past.

C.O WAS SITTING IN HIS YARD UPSET about his time in prison, and at the idea of his only son not knowing who he was.

He replayed his conversation with Teflon over and over in his head.

It was heavy on his mind, especially what his brother had told him about picking up on the lost time with his son, and not worrying about Cristal.

He knew getting over her would be hard.

He'd spent five years in the state pen, and every day until he'd maxed out, she'd been on his mind.

He loved her, and not worrying about her wouldn't be as easy as his brother thought.

Teflon had been right about his leaving her behind to raise their child all alone. The thing he wanted most was to get his family back and forget about the hurt she'd caused him—and the hurt he'd caused her.

Thoughts of her being with another man made his head light.

He hated the feeling! He got up and walked around to get himself together.

Not having money in his pocket stressed him out even more.

He wanted to spend time with Tahshawn, but it wouldn't have been right as a father to be around his son with no money to spend.

He wanted to put a smile on his son's face.

He sat back down and tried to come up with a good excuse to get money from his mother and father.

Being on house arrest for ninety days wasn't going to get the best of him.

He needed money, and he needed it fast.

He knew that a man without money had no opportunity to do anything he wishes.

But a man who has money have opportunities to do whatever.

For five years of his life, C.O hadn't had much of an opportunity.

Now that he was a free man back on the streets, he knew his chance for opportunity was around the corner.

"Hey boy, what you doing sitting here?"

The voice broke his thoughts.

When he turned around to see who it was, he jumped up out of his chair for a hug.

"Oh shit. Kim, what's up, cuzo? When you came home?" C.O asked.

"Boy, I came home Friday, on the first."

Kim had gained weight over the years while in prison, and it made her look years younger.

"When you came home?" She waited for his response in return.

"That's crazy, man, 'cause I maxed out on the first too.

And these pigs got me on ninety days of house arrest after I gave their asses five fucking years of my life."

As a free man, C.O felt trapped in a box.

"Isn't that some shit, man? I can't go nowhere." He pouted.

"If you can do five years, you can do ninety days.

Would you rather be locked up at home or up that road, doing hard time?"

Kim asked her cousin knowing he'd rather be home on house arrest instead of being in prison.

"Trust me. I ain't mad my nigga.

You know how many nights I prayed to be locked in my house instead of being locked up in prison? I got what I prayed for, so I'm cool.

And you need to throw those fucking state boots away."

He hadn't expected anyone to wear state-prison boots while being free. It made him want to yank Kim by the legs and cut the worn-down boots from her feet.

"If you're going to wear them bullshits, you need to give me fifty feet.

As a matter of fact, give me fifty states and a country."

They both laughed and hugged each other once more.

She was happy to see her little cousin after so many years.

Right before he been sent to prison, she'd witnessed the drug bust he got caught up in.

It had hurt her the most.

Even though she smoked crack, he would have given Kim anything.

He made sure she had food to eat and clothes on her back in the winter.

They noticed a car pull up in the driveway. It was their cousin Freaky Ty.

He was smoking a blunt that made C.O's eyes grow as wide as two silver dollars.

Right away, he reached for the blunt before even saying anything to his cousin.

He and Freaky Ty had had words in the past after C.O fucked his girlfriend, and the bond between them wasn't strong.

They gave each other daps, and that was about it.

Freaky Ty hugged Kim and then reached into his pocket and handed her a fifty-dollar bill so she could have money in her pocket.

"That's all I got on me right now Kim.

But if you catch me later, I should be able to toss you more, okay?"

He glanced over at C.O and felt a bit guilty about not giving him anything, so he tossed him a bag of loud.

C.O saw all the bullshit coming from his cousin. He had what he called, prison intuition.

He kept his mouth closed.

"Good looking, Freaky Ty. Is this what we're smoking now?"

C.O kept pulling on the blunt of loud his cousin had passed him.

"Yeah, it's the same shit. How you like it?"

Freaky Ty watched him smoke the best loud that came through his hands and waited for C.O to respond.

"It's good, but you know, anything will get me high right now.

Hell, this is my first blunt since I came home."

Freaky Ty glanced down at the black box around his cousin's ankle.

"What the fuck is that around your ankle?"

Freaky Ty and their cousin Kim both looked down at the monitor box wrapped around C.O's ankle.

"Oh, I'm on house arrest," he said.

"You're on house arrest, getting high?"

Freaky Ty questioned him.

C.O shrugged as if he didn't give two shits about the monitoring box.

"Freaky Ty chill my dude. I got this!

A few cups of warm water before I go see my probation officer, and I'm cool."

Kim and Freaky Ty watched C.O pull on the blunt, which later went out. They laughed at him.

"I hope you know what you're doing C.O don't fuck up.

Well, I just came by to check on y'all, I'm 'bout to bounce. I got shit to handle."

He gave Kim another hug and dapped C.O before he got in his car and left.

Kim shook her head in disbelief.

"Freaky Ty is full of shit. He's pushing all that heroin like people don't know what the hell he's selling.

Why is he going to give me fifty dollars and hand you a bag of weed like that's going to help you?"

C.O just smiled. "Man, fuck him, I don't need his money.

Hell, I can get my own fucking money.

He must have really forgotten I'm a go-getta." He spoke with pride.

"Yeah, I know! I'm just saying. All that money our cheap-ass cousin has."

She felt bad for her cousin C.O but knew he'll be alright.

"Kim, I know what the hell you're saying. Trust me. I'm cool, though. Mama and Daddy told me whenever they get back from the store, they're going to toss me forty dollars anyway, so there's nothing to sweat."

Kim could tell he was upset, so she let him have the last word.

"As a matter of fact, that's my mama and daddy right there."

Looking behind her, Kim heard her aunt Gayle yelling from inside the car.

Her aunt was happy to see Kim.

As soon as the car stopped, Kim pulled the door open to hug her aunt and uncle.

They all smiled and laughed at the weight she'd gained while she was in prison for two years.

Later, C.O walked into his mother and father's house to grab something to eat. All he ever ate was wheat bread with a glass water.

He'd become a vegetarian while serving his five years in prison, and now that he was home again, he hadn't found an appetite for anything besides wheat, grains, vegetables, fish, and chicken.

Man, they need to come on yo! He thought to himself.

Moments later, his father came into the house and handed him forty dollars.

"That's the best me and ya mother can do. So you better spend your money wisely."

C.O grabbed the money. It felt foreign since he hadn't felt money in a long time, and he shook his daddy's hand.

He later walked away, heading back outside thinking about his next move.

He kept the forty dollars in his hands, folding and unfolding it.

Then he rolled it, unrolled it, and put it in his pocket.

He tried to think of someone he could call to buy his first gram of crack, but he didn't have anybody's number to call.

He had to wait until one of his homeboys stopped, by before he could cop any dope.

He sat in a chair and watched Kim and his mother gossip about Kim doing the right thing with her life.

But with the type of plans he had in mind, Kim would be his only help at getting there, regardless of what his mother told her.

"Kim, I think I'm going to get back into the game and give it a second chance.

I want to be able to provide for my son," he told her later.

"Boy you just got out of the pen, and getting a job should be the only thing on your mind right now."

She tried her best to convince her cousin.

"Yeah, you're right about the job and all, but Kim, how long would that last? Getting a paycheck for four hundred dollars a week isn't shit.

Plus, most companies won't hire mothafuckas like us with fucked-up records, and if they do, they'll pay under the table just to protect their asses.

Then what, Kim? Then we won't be able to file taxes at the end of the year."

He paused to gain control over his high.

The blunt he'd smoked from Freaky Ty was kicking in even more.

"When we get old, neither one of us would be able to file for unemployment or Social Security. Cause we're not in the system as tax payers."

She felt he'd made a valid point, but she didn't want to take chances with her freedom again.

"How long have you thought about this?" she asked.

"Kim, to be honest, before I came home!"

He insured her...

She had no choice but to respect his mind; he kept it real.

Most people waited until they maxed out to think about getting back into the game, but with her cousin C.O it didn't work that way.

"Look, if that's what you want to do, then I can't stop you.

You're a grown-ass man now.

You're wise enough to make your own choices!

All I can tell you is to be careful. Them streets don't love you.

I don't care how much love you have for them streets. Just know the street isn't God to love.

It doesn't give life; it takes it."

For a second, he thought about what she'd said.

It made a lot of sense.

He knew the streets has wicked ways—the spells of cops, stickup kids, killers, haters, snitches, and drug pushers.

But the rush of it all had him trapped.

He had second thoughts about not going back to the streets, after a quick flash of him being back in prison flashed before his eyes.

But he was determined!

He had his plans all figured out, but what bothered him the most was his desire to find out who his baby mother was fucking, if she was fucking.

He wanted to know if dude was in the game or had an honest paying job.

He truly didn't care what he did to get money. He just wanted to know his worth.

"Kim, hear me out. I know you're trying to do right and all, but to be honest, I need your help."

He pleaded sadly.

"What you mean you need my help?"

He closed his eyes before continuing. He wanted his plans to sound convincing to her.

"Fuck it. Look man, if I get the work, can you be my runner?" he asked, being straightforward with her. He had no more time to waste.

"Damn, boy, you haven't heard not one word I just told you." She couldn't believe what her cousin had asked of her.

"Man, I heard every word Kim, but at least hear me out.

Between the both of us, we only have ninety fucking dollars. How long do you think your fifty dollars will last you, Kim? I'm saying, man, how fast you think it's going to take you to find a fucking job without all the red tape?"

He wanted her to see the bigger picture.

"Kim, at least help me until you find a job.

I'll keep money in your pocket until you find one, so you won't need or want for anything. You feel me?"

She stared him in the face and knew what he was saying could be true.

Finding a job wouldn't be as easy as it sounded, unless it was a side hustle getting paid twenty or maybe thirty dollars every other day.

"And you're going to do this on house arrest?" she asked.

"Kim, I got less than ninety days to do this shit, man."

He spoke aggressively with a determined look on his face, hoping she wouldn't back out.

"I don't know about this one, man." She doubted the idea.

"Hear me out. I got this shit mapped out.

I did the math on this house-arrest shit. The monitor box is set up at our grandmother's house, on her phone, and they gave me one hundred fifty feet to roam from the box.

That means I could move closer to the block. Think about it. I don't even stay at Grandmama's house.

And that's where the monitor box is at. I'm staying at home with my mama and daddy.

I just told my probation officer I was going to live at Grandmama's house 'cause I needed a place that has a phone, so they could hook the box up."

While he explained his plans, she saw the excitement in her little cousin's eyes.

The game to C.O was like an Xbox game to a teenage kid. She couldn't help but smile at him.

"C.O what are you saying?" Kim asked.

"Look, here's what I'm saying.

A while back, Daddy told me that our house is fifty feet away from Grandmama's house.

So that means I have a hundred more feet to play with.

All I need to do is get in front of our house, cause I can't push dope right here for Grandma to see, Kim.

She's always sitting on the front porch, and I need to move from this spot."

He spoke in a low tone, hoping no one was able to get a drop on his plans.

"So what do you need me to do?"

She couldn't tell him no; she knew what the dope game meant to him.

He was in too deep!

She knew her cousin ate, slept, and shit the dope game every since he was a kid.

Hell she were the one who taught him about the crack game when was only fifteen years old.

"I need you to go stand by the telephone and keep your eyes on the monitoring box.

It has a light on it, a red and green.

Right now, the light should be on green. I'm going to walk around the front of our house.

If the light on the box turns red, call me. That means I'm out of bounds. But let's pray that shit won't happen.

I need to get in front of our house, Kim."

"If your daddy told you the houses are fifty feet apart and you got one hundred fifty feet to roam away from the box, then you should be able to go around the front of y'all's house."

He exhaled deeply. "Kim, I know that.

I just need to be safe and sure."

He stood up to face her, they both smiled.

"All right then."

She went to their grandmother's house and kept her eyes on the monitor box as he went around their house.

As expected, the light stayed on green.

He was ready to open up shop.

He pulled out a lawn chair and sat in his new spot. He busted a blunt and rolled the bag of weed his cousin Freaky Ty had given him.

Moments later, Kim came walking up from behind.

She looked at him and shook her head as if he were crazy.

She knew that once he had his mind set to do anything, there was nothing anyone could do to change that, let alone stop him.

"Boy, you know your daddy is going to flip if he sees us in his yard like this!"

Kim looked around in search for her uncle Dennis, not wanting to get fussed at.

"Girl, we good right now. Hell, he's happy to see us home, so he's going to be cool."

They laughed at the events that's about to take course.

"So who are you going to buy the dope from, all you got is forty dollars?

What you going to get with that?" Kim asked,

"I'm buying a gram, and watch how I bounce back Kim. Watch me now."

She knew he was a hustler, but coming up with just one gram of crack? She had to see it to believe it.

This nigga is tripping! Kim thought.

They paused when a black Chrysler 300 pulled up in their driveway. Their cousins Punch and Black jumped out of the car with bottles of Patrón Silver and Red Bull in their hands. They'd come to drink and get high.

But when C.O saw them, the only thing that ran through his mind was spending his forty dollars to buy a gram.

He was ready to get down to business.

He smoked the weed and passed the bottle of Patrón to Kim.

She was more into drinking than smoking weed anyway.

"Yo, Punch, I want one of y'all to sell me a gram, man." C.O had a straightforward look on his face.

Punch smiled but pointed at Black.

"You'll have to holla at that nigga. All I got left is a ball."

C.O sucked his teeth and shook his head as if Punch were a disgrace to the game.

"Damn, y'all niggas in a Chrysler 300 with bottles of Patrón, and all you got is a ball? Man, Black, sell me a gram, dawg."

His boy Black just sat on the hood of the rental car he drove and laughed.

He knew Punch felt played by the statement because the night before, Punch had been in club Isis, throwing dollar bills as if he were big meech.

"I got you, nigga." Black went into his car to grab the bag of dope and then handed it to C.O.

He looked at Kim to see her reaction, and she looked readier than he'd thought.

"My brother Freaky Ty told me you and Kim was home, so me and Black had to come check y'all out.

We were heading to Pawleys Island when he called us."

Punch was always the playing type of person who showed no threat to anyone. All he wanted to do was smoke weed and laugh all day.

"Yeah, Freaky Ty stopped by to holla at me and Kim for a quick minute. But he had shit he needed to do, so he couldn't stay long."

C.O made small talk with them, but the only thing on his mind was getting his money right.

Y'all niggas faking. I'm 'bout to bypass you niggas on this dope shit.

Every night, y'all are in the clubs, buying weed and getting rentals like y'all got it like that.

Don't worry. All y'all clowns will soon be buying from me.

The thoughts played in his mind therapeutically.

While they were sitting and talking, a purple 2002 Honda Accord pulled into the club parking lot across from his yard.

They noticed a white lady in the driver's seat.

She rolled the passenger window down, and right away, Punch recognized her.

"Oh shit, that's a sale!"

He ran to the window to serve her, but C.O yelled at his cousin.

"Hell nah! Let Kim make that run, nigga. Wasn't you and Black on the way to the Island?"

C.O gave Kim the whole gram so she could make their first sale.

"Kim tell her to give you her phone number, and you'll call her when we get more!"

He yelled out to her as she walked away.

"It's a different ball game, niggas. I'm home now!

All y'all had five years to get your bread right.

So get in that rental, and take a tour." C.O smiled a devilish smile.

He saw Kim give the smoker the dope after she received the money.

It's on, baby. That's right, Kim. Get that money!

"Hey, girl, what's your name? So when I see you again, I'll know," Kim asked.

"My name is Lisa. Do you have a phone number I can contact you on?

I don't want my husband to catch me coming down this street."

Lisa was the type of woman who came from money.

She owned the Palace Resort, which her family had handed down to her.

She'd become a victim of smoking crack when she moved to Myrtle Beach from Miami, Florida.

"Nah, as a matter of fact, let me get your number.

And I'll call you as soon as I get one," Kim told her.

"Okay, well, here's my number where you can reach me.

Do you think you'll be able to get more of these? Hell, I'll be needing more in a few.

I'm at some friend's house. We'll definitely be looking to get more in a few."

Lisa placed an early order through Kim. She needed a steady supplier.

"Well, my name is Lady Bug, and I'll call you in the next half hour, okay?"

They shook hands to seal their future deals.

"Lady Bug, make it an hour because I have to stop a few places before getting back to my friend's house.

And if you see a white guy driving a green construction truck, that's my husband.

If he comes through here asking if y'all seen me, please tell him no, all right?" Lisa winked at Kim.

"I got you."

Kim rushed back to where C.O was standing and handed him a hundred-dollar bill.

He turned to his boy Black with the money in his hand.

This time, he bought two grams.

"C.O I'ma put you onto my people, 'cause I can't give deals all the time."

Black informed him...

C .O DIDN'T GET ANOTHER PACKAGE
until midnight.
He flipped the hundred dollars
he'd made that day and bought a ball of
crack from a connection given to him by his
boy Black.

Man Man was one of Myrtle Beach Police Department's biggest problems.

He was a true hard-core gangsta who kept it one hundred with his crew, selling anything that pulled in money: X pills, heroin, crack, and cocaine.

If niggas wanted to fuck, he pimped hos too.

When they first met, they got right down to business.

Afterward, they talked and laughed as if they'd always known each other.

"My nigga Black told me about you.

I told him I was coming to holla at you."

Man Man had a smooth complexion.

He was a dark-skinned young brother who stood five foot nine.

The minute he laid eyes on C.O, he knew by the way he talked that C.O was about his money, and that made Man Man become attached.

"That's what it is, my dude. To be honest, he told me about you too.

I just hope you got what I want, when I want it at all times.

I'll show you what I'm about. I was gone for a while, but I'm here now.

Fuck what you heard. You can get a first-class flight to see what I'm doing, my nigga."

Man Man laughed.

"I got you. When did you get out?"

Although Man Man had a killer personality, he dressed as if he were the college type.

People barely saw him; he lived his life like a hunted animal.

He always watched his every move.

"I got out a few days ago, and now I'm out here paper-chasin', trying to catch up.

You feel me? So what you got for me?"

"Black told me you wanted a ball, right?"

Man man asked while retrieving the bag of crack from the console.

"Yeah, but you'll let me cop the ball for a hundred?"

C.O asked, hoping Man Man wouldn't let him down.

"My nigga, you good.

Hell, I know you just got out and need the help right now.

Bra, I'm with the struggle. I'm not here to oppress you.

I want to see you grow financially out here in these streets, nigga."

Man Man smiled to show his crush-diamond grills.

He glided his right hand across his shiny, wavy head to smooth out his wave.

He knew he was the fliest killa in town.

"Damn, my dude, that's love, and trust me. I got you as soon as I get on my feet."

C.O reached out for a handshake.

When he was younger, his daddy had told him, If a man shakes your hand with a tight grip, it'll show he's a good businessman.

And it'll show his trust in you.

But if a man shows hesitation in a light grip of a handshake, it means he is not sure he wants to do business with you.

He doesn't trust you!

Off the rip, put it in your mind that he is bad for business.

Automatically, he is going to try to slime ball you.

With great approval, C.O didn't feel any hesitation in Man Man handshake.

He neither felt nor saw anything soft about him.

Everything about the nigga was tight, from his 360 waves to his tight handshake.

"Nah, you good. I just want to see you get on my nigga.

Word, but we'll have to politic some other time. I got to head back to the beach.

I got other people to see. But I'ma get back at you, though."

They gave each other daps before Man Man walked toward his candy-apple-red Yukon.

After he got into his truck, he slid down the dark tinted window and tossed an ounce of purple haze to a real nigga.

"Try it out!" Man Man yelled, and then he backed out of the driveway.

Right away, C.O ran to his grandmother's house to call his first soon-to-be client.

As he took off running, Kim yelled to remind him to let the lady know, she had dealt with a girl named Lady Bug earlier.

When he tried to dial the number, he had to hang up and redial it twice.

He was overly excited and determined to make his next sale.

After he made the call, he went back outside and waited.

"C.O you got through to her?" Kim asked.

"Yep, I told her that Lady Bug said to come through. She'll be here in about thirty minutes."

He shook the white crack rock out into his sweaty palm.

He was now back in the game, knee deep, and loved the feeling.

"You need to get you a phone because you can't be calling them feins off Grandma's phone." She warns him.

Whenever he saw Kim point her finger at him or even someone else, he knew she wasn't playing.

"Trust me. I got this, man."

Kim reached into her pocket to get a lighter to spark the half cigarette she was holding behind her ear.

Moments later, they saw a purple Honda pull up.

"Oh shit, Kim that's ole girl! Here go the dope."

He poured the crack into her hand.

"Hold on, C.O Damn, slow down. I need to know how much she want,"

Kim yelled at him with her arm stretched out, and with her palm open.

"She wants the whole thing, Kim. I told her three hundred dollars."

Kim ran over to make the sale and counted the money while she sat in the fein's car.

"Hey, Lady Bug, when you think y'all will be able to have that ounce I needed, 'Cause I don't like coming back and forth in this area."

Lisa pinched a small piece of crack from the ball of dope she'd just bought.

She placed the crack in a stem to smoke while waiting for Kim's answer.

"Baby, you'll just have to work with us. Trust me. We'll have it for you soon. Just keep spending your money with us."

After seeing Lisa hit the stem, Kim inhaled the thick cloud of smoke through her nose.

The smell of it made her want to ask for a hit. But she had to be strong at not going back to getting high.

"Oh, I don't mind spending the money. Y'all just need more stuff."

Lisa eyes were wide from the crack she just smoked.

"Trust me. We will have it," Kim said.

"Well, Lady Bug, talk to you later. Call me!"

After making the sale, Kim walked back over to where her cousin was sitting.

"Here go the money, and you got to do something quick about getting more dope."

Kim's stomach bubbled up from the sweet smell of crack that had invaded her nose. Her mouth watered.

I need me a hit now. Kim thought!

"Why you say that?"

C.O asked while sniffing the three crisp hundred-dollar bills.

"'Cause the bitch really wants to buy an ounce and not grams and balls." Kim paused.

"You got to understand, C.O the bitch got money, and she don't want to keep coming back and forth on the block to get trapped off with sled cause you know this block is hot, and lose everything."

He thought about what Kim was telling him. It made sense.

"Yeah, you're right. As a matter of fact, I'm about to call Man Man now so I can get straight with more shit."

He went back to his grandmother's house to call his supplier right away.

He didn't want to miss out on any chances to make a dollar.

"Hello? Who's this?"

Man Man answered his phone with Blood Raw music blasting in the background.

"Yo, Man Man, this C.O!"

he yelled through the receiver.

"What's good, my nigga? You trying to see me?"

C.O slightly bobbed his head to the music.

"Hell yeah, where you at on the beach?"

While waiting for Man Man's response, he soaked in the words of the rapper everyone mistook for Jezzy or Yo Gotti.

"Nah, I'm on Atlantic Beach, but I'll swing through.

What you trying to get?" Man Man asked.

"I got three hundred!" C.O spoke with pride now.

"I'll tell you what, my nigga.

I'll throw you a half ounce for that. 'Cause I see you trying your best to get back on."

C.O couldn't believe this nigga he'd just met was about to bless him with such a sweet deal.

"Man Man, do me a favor: go ahead and bring an ounce with that half.

'Cause as soon as you leave, I'll be calling you back for that anyway."

He wanted to show Man Man what type of hustle game he have.

He was all about spending every dime of his money whenever he flipped his bread.

When he was younger, the feins in his hood had taught him something of value.

They'd told him not to cheat himself and to spend all the money he had on dope.

He'd never go broke!

If you got dope, you got money. They'd told C.O, only a fool would think he'll go broke by spending all his money on dope.

"Damn, Mr. Grand Hustler, all right,"

Man Man said smiling on the other end of the line.

"I got you my nigga. Give me an hour, and I'll be there."

C.O hung the phone up and then walked back to where Kim was still sitting.

He couldn't help but smile, he now, was back on his grind.

His house arrest might stop him from hitting the streets to get pussy, but it wouldn't stop him from getting his money.

The minute he sat back down in the chair, he saw his daddy and mama pull into the yard.

He and Kim stared at each other. They knew they had it coming to them.

"All right, I'ma tell y'all right now: don't make that a habit, sitting in my front yard.

I'm trying to grow my grass back."

His father spoke with a calm tone that surprised them.

"Daddy, the reason why I came to sit here is because I'm tired of sitting in the backyard," C.O said.

"Well, I don't want no paper in my yard, Corey."

C.O looked over at Kim and stuck his tongue out at her. "Okay, Daddy."

Without saying anything else, his father walked away.

"I told you he wasn't going to trip."

Not long after Man Man left, Redeyes and Grouch pulled up in an F-150 truck with their music playing. Me and My Brother, by the Ying Yang Twins.

Everyone called them the Newport Twins. They looked a lot alike. Redeyes was the baby from all his brothers, and Grouch was the knee baby.

C.O smiled. He couldn't believe he was seeing his two little brothers at an older age.

Look at my li'l' brothers, he thought.

Before he'd gone to prison, Redeyes and Grouch had been young and not knowing shit about driving. Not only did the driving surprise him, but seeing them drink and smoke blew his mind.

The sight of it all, kind of made him angry, but he had to realize, they had grown up over the years—and fast!

When his two little brothers got out of the truck, he first noticed the smiles he remembered from when they were younger boys.

Redeyes reached out to hug his big brother while Grouch hugged Kim.

"Damn, y'all grew the fuck up, man," He said with a Surprising tone.

"C.O what the fuck you expect? That we'll stay little and young forever?"

Redeyes smiled and looked his brother up and down to get a better look at him.

He stepped back so Grouch would have the chance to embrace their long-lost big brother as well.

"Yo, Kim, look at these niggas, man." C.O laughed at the sight of his little brothers becoming men.

"I know, right? They grew up like hell, man," Kim laughed out loud.

While they all were enjoying the moment, they saw the purple Honda and six more cars pull up.

"Yo, Kim, I' ma go in the house to keep an eye on Mama and Daddy while you take care of those sales.

We'll have to be very low key about this shit."

He didn't want his mama or daddy seeing them making any drug transactions.

He needed to keep a good face with them.

After all, both him and Kim had been released from prison only a few days ago.

"Don't let your daddy and them catch me doing this shit," she begged her cousin.

"Kim, I got you."

Redeyes and Grouch were shocked at what they were seeing.

They couldn't believe their brother was back in the game that soon.

Redeyes looked at Grouch with a smile.

"Yo, Grouch, don't tell me that nigga is back in the game already!"

They watched Kim make the sale.

To help the situation, they even watched the highway to keep an eye out for the cops.

"Redeyes, guess what?" Grouch smiled.

"What's up?" Redeyes waited for his brother to speak.

"I'm moving back home," Grouch told him.

"Fuck that. I'm moving back home too.

These niggas is about to go broke out here.

Everybody knows what our brother is about."

Redeyes looked at Grouch and then back at the sales Kim was dealing with.

"Fuck that shit, Grouch. He going to fuck with us. Watch."

Redeyes pulled a pack of cigarettes from his pocket.

He handed his brother a Newport as well. "Let me get a light, stupid nigga," Redeyes teased.

Kim returned with the money in her hand and then looked over at Grouch and asked for a Newport.

"Yo, Kim, let me ask you a question man. How much money did they spend?"

Kim just smiled.

"All I got to say is this... The Hot Road is about to be booming."

C.O came back outside with a cup of water and four slices of wheat bread in his hands.

Redeyes and Grouch stared at each other and smiled.

They knew it was about to be on.

"Here go all the money I just made." Kim handed over the money to her cousin.

"Thanks, Kim." Right away, C.O began counting his money.

"Well, I'm about to walk across the street to see Hellen, I haven't seen her since I came home."

She shook her head smiling at her cousin because she knew C.O only had one thing on his mind.

And that was to come up.

Without looking up, he waved his hand that held the money she'd just made him.

"That's what's up, Kim. Tell her I asked about her too.

But, Kim, please come back man. You know I need you out here with me."

Kim stuck her thumbs up and walked off in the direction of Hellen's.

Hellen, a kindhearted woman, was there grandmother's best friend. She sold chili hot dogs, fish, and chicken sandwiches to the people in the hood.

She had a son name Biggie who'd grown up with C.O and Teflon as kids.

While C.O was serving his five years in the state pen, his boy Biggie had gotten caught by the feds.

It was Biggie's first time ever doing time.

He was sentenced to twelve years and had to do 85 percent of his time. C.O had been at Campbell Pre-Work Release Center in

Columbia, South Carolina, when he called home and heard about Biggie and the rest of his crew who'd gotten hit by the feds.

Biggie was the only one who'd taken his shit like a G. Everyone else had told everything they knew.

He shook his head at the thought of the ones he'd believed were real who'd folded under federal pressure.

It had made him lose a lot of respect for them.

"Grouch, y'all know what I'm thinking about?"

C.O paused for a moment before speaking again.

"If I never had gone to state prison, I think I would have been doing fed time right now."

He spoke with a distant look in his eyes.

"Why you say that?" asked Grouch.

"Dawg, think about it. The only fucking person that didn't snitch was Biggie. Everybody else ran their mouth." He sucked his teeth in a disgusted manner.

"You right, 'cause I heard Beans was the main one. And the dumbass nigga caused his own little fuckup," Grouch said.

"That's what I'm saying. So how in the hell you going to cop six bricks of coke in a 4.6 Range Rover sitting on twenty-four-inch chrome rims?"

C.O looked over to Redeyes as if he could answer his question.

Instead Redeyes just shrugged his shoulders.

Redeyes and Grouch then looked behind them to see what C.O was looking at.

The next thing they knew, they heard someone yelling for him.

"Who the fuck is that calling my name?" C.O felt a bit confused and nervous.

"Man, that's Lex," Redeyes told him.

Lex was one of the upscale dope boys who'd become a member of the crack-pipe users while C.O was in prison.

Teflon had written to him about Lex becoming a crackhead.

Lex had had a Mazda Millennium and a 1200 Ninja motorcycle. He'd sold it for a little of nothing!

But there was only one way to find out if the rumor was true to look for the crackhead signs.

"Lex, what's up, man?" He greeted Lex with a welcoming heart.

Lex smiled,

"I heard you been out, so I just came by to check you out before I went to work."

C.O noticed that Lex no longer looked like himself. He'd lost a lot of weight, and his head was nappy as hell.

"Damn, Lex, where you work at?"

Lex looked down at the ground with embarrassment.

"I work at the K and W Cafeteria, behind the Inlet Square Mall."

He spoke with insecurities.

"So who told you I was home?" C.O asked, and he waited for Lex to respond.

"Shit, I saw Kim. She told me you was back out." Lex smiled, showing his now beige teeth.

C.O felt bad for him.

He wanted to know what had gone wrong with Lex. Why had he started smoking crack?

"Where you saw Kim? I was waiting for her all fuckin day, yo."

He became angry at his cousin for not being back on time.

"I saw her over at Whitehead's house. If you give me a hit, I'll go get her."

C.O was caught by surprise when he said Whitehead's name. Whitehead definitely got high.

"Is that where Kim at Lex? Her ass supposed to been back hours ago.

She told me she was going to see Biggie's mama, Hellen.

And she's at Whitehead's spot? Lex please tell Kim I need her dawg."

C.O could not believe Lex and his downfall.

"Say no more," Lex said, and with that, he left.

"C.O I know you heard Lex ask you for a hit," Redeyes asked.

He looked over at his little brother and shook his head.

"Yeah, I heard him. And what the hell that supposed to mean? I'm not giving that weak-ass nigga shit."

He realized many things had changed over the years while he was away.

4

S ALES WERE BACK TO BACK, AND C.O felt good about the progress he'd made in his first two months back home.

Not only was Kim running for him, but he also had let his two younger brothers talk him into letting them run for him.

He did not like the idea, but he'd rather they ran for him than someone else.

He was surprised by how they handled their business. It was like they had it in their blood to be a hustler.

He remembered many nights in the past when he'd come home in the middle of the night and found them sleeping in the same bed, resting for school the next morning, he would go in their room and hide the money he'd made all that day and most of that night in the floor vent.

When he'd leave, his little brothers would sneak a peek at his stash.

They always had wanted to be like their brother. He lived by his own rules, and their mother and father never gave him a hard time.

C.O was a true thug in their eyes.

They knew because of him and their brother Teflon, no one would fuck with them.

Everyone knew who their big brothers was, and putting hands on Grouch and Redeyes would have been crossing a line of disrespect.

No one was foolish enough to do so, and they took full advantage of the respect and went wild.

C.O looked at his son and smiled.

Tahshawn was running back and forth, spraying a frog with the supersoaker water gun his father had bought him.

COREY N. SMALLS

C.O looked into the oak tree above him, which was covered in moss.

He asked God to please watch over him while he was out chasing money.

The Hot Road was booming by the minute and he knew that sled probably gotten the word by now about him back supplying the hood with drugs, but still, he didn't give a fuck.

The nickname Hot Road had been used since the late seventies or early eighties.

A lot of old-time drug pushers and pimps roamed that street to make their ends meet.

But now it was the end of the old and the start of the new, cause C.O were the new landlord in town.

"Daddy, can we go to the park? I want to get on the slide,"

His son asked with a wide smile on his face. It made his father smile as well cause he couldn't believe that he have a son of his own.

"P. T we can go, but we'll have to be back real soon yo.

It's almost three o'clock, and I'm not allowed to be out of reach from the monitor box, okay?"

That day was the first time they'd actually spent time together.

Being around his son made him feel complete, although he'd missed four years of his son growing up, he had plans to make things up, just like Teflon had told him to.

"Okay daddy, and why you always call me P.T?"

He smiled. "I call you P.T because you eat a lot of Pop-Tarts, nigga."

His son balled up his small fist and held it up at his father.

"Daddy, I don't like that name."

C.O reached for him and began tickling him all over.

"What you gonna do, lil' nigga huh? I see you got your fist up."

He tickled and squeezed Tahshawn playfully.

"Stop, Daddy. Stop! You're tickling me." His son laughed uncontrollably.

Hearing Tahshawn call him Daddy made his day.

Damn, he just called me Daddy for the third time!

"Well...Stop eating all them Pop-Tarts, and I won't call you P.T"

They were now forehead to forehead.

"But, Daddy, I love Pop-Tarts. That's why I eat them." His son pouted playfully.

"Well, then I'ma keep calling you P.T," he teased.

"Daddy, I'ma call you Boob if you don't stop it."

He gave Tahshawn a confusing stare. He wanted to laugh.

He hadn't expect his son to say a word that made him think of a female body part.

"Boob! Tahshawn, where'd you get that from?" He looked at his son for a minute.

He wanted to ask him a question—a question he needed his son to answer—but he knew it would be wrong to pull his son into his and Cristal's problems.

But he really wanted to know.

"Tahshawn, look at me. You know that I love you, right? And I really want you to know that, I am so sorry for leaving you and your mother behind, when I went to prison."

C.O waited a moment before continuing.

"Daddy, what is prison?" Tahshawn asked.

"Son, look at me for a second.

Prison is a place for bad boys and girls.

I've done bad things in the past, and that's where I went."

He rubbed the sweat from his forehead. "Tahshawn, listen. I need to ask you something."

God, please forgive me for doing this. But I need to know!

His son just stared at him as if he had done something wrong.

"Son, have you ever saw your mother with a boyfriend?"

Tahshawn got quiet. He remembered his mother telling him not to tell his daddy her business. Not saying another word, Tahshawn just stood there looking stuck.

"Tahshawn, I promise I'm not going to tell your mother if you tell me what I want to know.

You're my son. My life, pride, and joy. I'll never betray you."

Like your mother done me.

"I promise you that, okay?" He made a pinkie promise with his son.

Right after that, Tahshawn told him everything.

"Daddy, will you and Mommy get married one day?"

Getting married to Cristal was something he'd always wanted.

Having a family with her and their son would have made him a complete man.

"Son, I have always prayed for that, but me and your mother have some huge issues to fix first, okay?"

He closed his eyes and saw the long, bloody journey ahead of him to get his love back.

Hustlin' from the bottom and getting it out of the mud for the thing he loved the most.

'Granddaddy, how do you know when you're in love?'

'Corey, son, let me tell you something.

One day when you're older, I promise you'll know it!

True love will make you do things you don't have an answer for.

It'll control you physically and mentally.

It'll make you do emotional and magical things your heart won't be able to control.'

The conversation with his grandfather played in his mind.

He'd been only seven years old at the time.

Now that he was twenty-four years old, he felt the feeling his grandfather had told him about love.

"Mmm, okay then, well... Can we go to the park now daddy?" Tahshawn asked.

"Yeah, but let's race there."

Before they left to go to the park, he told his brothers to come to the playground if they ran out of crack, then he went into the house and grabbed a bottle of Deer Park water for him and his son to drink.

"Okay, P.T on your mark. Get set."

Before he had the chance to say Go, his son took off running.

C.O ran slowly, pretending he was running his hardest so his son could keep the lead.

He was having a lot of fun with his son, and they both enjoyed every second of it.

Cristal was in her apartment, getting ready to go out to the club. She called her homegirl to see if she had any plans for the night.

There was a new club on the boulevard that everyone went to, Club Myst, and she wanted to go out and let her wild side out.

"Hey, girl, what's your whoring ass doing tonight? I sure hope you ain't staying in the house and watching reruns."

"Cristal, what's up, girl?" Candi sounded as if she were about to go to sleep, but her girl had called in time before she went to bed.

"Candi, let's go out tonight. It's Memorial Day weekend, and Club Myst got this blue-carpet affair thing going on."

Cristal spoke excitedly to convince her homegirl to roll with her.

"Girl, I heard about that," Candi said excitedly.

"Girl, they got a crank-dat-Roy contest, swag, and surfin' contest. They have the stanky-leg contest and walk-it-out contest.

It's going to be the crunkest party on the ocean, girl."

Candi thought about what she should wear if she went out to Club Myst.

A lot of big-time ballers would be in that spot tonight.

She had to look good and feel sexy at the same time.

She had the body to pose in a straight stuntin' magazine.

Her body measurements were 34-28-47.

She was Creole, Portuguese and had moved to the South at the age of ten.

She loved Myrtle Beach and wouldn't have moved anywhere else in the world.

"Bitch, what are you wearing tonight?" Candi asked.

"Candi, girl, put it like this: damn near nothing. Just know I got to dress for the kill.

I want them drug boys' dicks to bust through their pants when they see me coming through.

Hell, Tahshawn is staying with his daddy for the weekend, so I'm free."

"Girl, Corey home?" Candi asked.

"Yes, child, and he needs to spend time with his damn son.

Hell, I raised him from a baby until now. I need a break."

"Cristal, what if Corey be at the club tonight?" Candi joked.

"Oh, hell no. His black ass better be at home with our son!" she yelled.

"Well, let me get ready then. I got to take a shower before I get dressed."

After they hung up with each other, Cristal went to the shower and began to soap her body down.

Her dark brown nipples stood straight up as thoughts of her baby daddy penetrated her mind.

She wanted to know if his sex was the same or better than the last time they'd made love.

In the past, he'd been the shit!

She could not get enough of him.

She started to pinch her nipples and lick them.

She ran her hands down her flat stomach until she reached her swollen clit.

With two soapy fingers, she rubbed her clit.

She eased her wet fingers into her silky hole until she reached her climax.

She came within minutes.

She finger-fucked her silky hole fast.

She leaned her head back while biting her lip; it felt too good.

She wanted Corey.

She needed him, but at the same time, she hated him.

When she was done, she felt a bit ashamed, looking around the shower as if eyes were staring at her.

She stepped out and dried off with a body towel.

That night, she put on a pink shirt pulled down low enough to reveal her smooth shoulders.

She wore a pink lace thong and no bra, with a pair of stilettos that had pink straps that wrapped up to her calves.

She had dressed to kill, but at the same time, being respectful about her shit.

Once dressed, she picked up her cell phone to call Candi. "Hey, girl, are you ready? 'Cause I'm 'bout to leave out."

"Yeah, girl, I'm ready. I got on my Tory Burch cocktail dress with my sexy stilettos.

And this dress better make wonders, 'cause I paid three hundred twenty-five dollars for it!" Candi cried playfully.

"Well, I'm on my way now, bitch."

She hung up the phone and then took a second look at herself before walking out the door.

Damn, I got it going on! I just got to remind myself not to bend over, 'cause my ass will be out there.

She applied her Baby Phat lip gloss, and after that, she was set to go.

When she got in her car, she called to check on Tahshawn, but when she heard her baby daddy answer the phone, her heart began to race, causing her to blush a little.

"Corey, what is Tahshawn doing?"

On the other end of the phone, C.O was smoking weed. He coughed.

"What you mean what's he doing? He's here chilling watching television."

"Corey, please don't have him up all damn night. It's already after twelve o'clock,"

Cristal spoke as if she were angry at him.

"First of all, it's the summertime, and he don't have to be at school tomorrow.

And he's my child too!

So don't be calling here and telling me what to do!" C.O yelled.

"Nigga, fuck you. Your ass better be fucking happy I let you get him."

Cristal tried her best to get under her baby daddy's skin, and she was loving it.

"Look, don't call here with the dumb shit, man.

Me and Tahshawn is in here laid back until you called just now."

He hated his baby mother and couldn't stand how she tried to play him whenever they talked.

"Well, let me speak to him, Corey." She heard him puffing on the blunt.

"No, you'll talk to him when he gets back home to you.

Just go to the club and whore around, 'cause that's your fucking plan anyway."

"I ain't no—"

Before she could get the last word out, she heard the dial tone on the other end of the line.

Damn, I hate that black son of a bitch. His broke ass!

I T WAS A NICE, COOL DAY WITH MILD weather.

C.O was sitting in his front yard reading the *XXL*, May issue, with Rick Ross on the front cover.

He wanted to know the deal on the beef between him and 50 Cent.

If anybody knew about anyone's beef in the industry, it was *XXL*.

He saw the facts in black and white on page 70, as part of the Rick Ross interview: 'Rick Ross, William Leonard Roberts II, was a correctional officer for eighteen months.'

He saw what Rick Ross had told the world: "I never tried to hide my past.

I never ratted on a nigga.

I never prosecuted a nigga.

I never locked a nigga up."

Right away, he felt where Rick Ross was coming from: it had only been a job.

He thought back to when he'd been housed at a correctional institution in South Carolina.

While there, he'd witnessed numerous officers bringing in weed, crack, cocaine, and cell phones into the system.

Although they have a job to do, the officers keep it gangsta for them niggas.

He told himself.

He flipped through the pages until he saw the eye-candy page.

Right away, he fell in love with a beautiful Nubian figure who caught his eye.

Damn, this bitch is bad!

Mia Milano made his dick grow hard as he stared at her ass shot. She had an amazing pose.

The way she was ripping the net of her bodysuit made her look a bit more desperate than he was.

He started to rub himself, until he noticed an all-black McLaren pull into his yard.

He notice his brother Teflon stepping out from the backseat dressed in a Sean John shirt, and jeans with Mauri gator shoes to match.

He was carrying a Louis Vuitton bag in his left hand while typing on his T-Mobile Sidekick LX with his right hand.

C.O then noticed two females in the front seat of his brother's car.

The girl in the passenger seat stepped out to wipe cigar tobacco off her lap. She was beautiful, and he wanted to meet her.

"Eh, Teflon!"

He called out to his brother.

"Let me holla at them beautiful ladies in your car fool."

Teflon just nodded to let him know it was cool.

Right away, he walked over to meet the ladies.

"Hi and how are y'all doing today?"

He was respectful to them. The girls looked at each other as if he were playing himself.

At first, he felt stupid about going over to meet them, but he had to go through with it now that he was there.

Fuck it. It is what it is! He told himself.

"Hey, boo, I'm fine, and you?" One of the females responded.

"I'm doing okay. What's your name?", he asked while staring into her eyes.

"My name is Felicia, and yours?" She was feeling him already because of his approach.

"Well, they call me Walt Diznee."

Felicia looked over towards her friend as if she were confused, and then back at him.

"I'm sorry. You said your name is Walt Disney, right?" She repeated his name with a questionable look on her face.

"Yeah, except my name is spelled D-i-z-n-e-e, not D-i-s-n-e-y," he wanted to be sure she had the spelling correct as well.

"How's that?" Poochie asked, cutting in.

Poochie and Felicia had been friends since college. She'd majored in business accounting and worked at Wells Fargo as an accountant for five years.

She was good with numbers.

And stood four foot three with a caramel skin tone, the very same complexion as his son's mother.

Her body was petite, with a cute plumb ass.

Poochie was half Cuban and half Hawaiian and was an independent type of woman who loved to see men beg for pussy.

"They call me Walt Diznee 'cause I'm about my business."

He kept a straight face. Without cracking a smile, he maintained his composure.

"I thought Disney was about fun and excitement," Felicia asked.

"Well, it is. It could be about as much excitement as you want it to be.

But the business begins with you and I trading numbers first.

And straight to the point, I want to be a part of what you have going on."

He had Felicia's full attention now. Like a king cobra, he had her dancing to his music.

"I hear you, Walt Diznee." She smiled.

"But don't you think it'd be wise to ask a girl if she has a man?"

C.O shrugged in a way to inform Felicia he didn't give a fuck if she had a man or not.

"To be honest Felicia, any man that ask a woman do she have a man, is either gay or a punk.

I'm not trying to meet him, boo, I'm trying to meet you.

I mean, if you can't see that, then maybe I need to walk around to the driver's side to talk with your friend. She's cute too," he teased.

"Well, if you think she's cute, how come you didn't walk straight to my homegirl?"

Felicia rolled her neck at him.

"Because your nose look cuter."

She'd never met anyone who would tell her crazy things to save her company.

She gave him ten points for the statement and began to pick at his brain.

"So tell me, Walt Diznee. Who are you to Mr. Teflon?" She pulled on her blunt and waited for his answer.

"Well, Teflon is my brother."

He spoke with pride, and knew by telling them that Teflon was his brother, he would be all the way in with them.

"He's your brother? I've been knowing Mr. Teflon for some years now, and not once have I seen you before."

He felt disappointed. He couldn't believe his brother had never told them about him.

"That's because I spent five years in prison.

And now that I'm home, I'm trying to find me someone of your height, size, looks, smell, and style.

And hopefully you'll feel the same way about me."

Felicia heard her girl whisper to her to give her number up.

"So you're fresh from the pen? Hmm, maybe you can use some excitement.

Will you allow me to assist you in that matter?" She teased him.

Felicia began to play mind games with him, not knowing he peeped game. So he played along.

Right away, she wrote her cell number on a piece of paper.

She opened the door and spread her legs apart revealing her pussy print to him.

She dropped the number between her soft, thick pecan-colored thighs.

She then saw his eyes follow.

He was hypnotized!

"Oops. Is it okay if you get that for me, Walt Diznee?" She spoke Without hesitation.

He reached for the number, and before he pulled away, he softly plucked her pussy with his middle finger.

It made her tingle all over. He'd caught her off guard.

He smiled at her, and quickly changed the subject to get her mind right.

"Nice heels. Who made them?"

She had to look down to remember the type of heels she was wearing.

"Thanks, and my shoes are by this designer named Steven. You like them?"

Before he could say anything else, he saw Teflon walking toward them.

Teflon gave him a dap and hopped back into the backseat of his McLaren.

Felicia blew him a kiss, and they pulled off.

C.O sat back down and thought about how big in the game Teflon had gotten.

And now, he's ready for his turn!

C̦

Teflon used to work for a restaurant called Drunken Jack's as a dishwasher.

And he was truly in love with his baby mother and did everything he could to keep her happy, until she up and left him one day for a nickel-and-dime street runner.

It hurt him to his heart that she just up and left him after all the hard work he had done to pay bills and put food on the table.

She felt it still wasn't enough for her.

She kept giving him a hard time because she wanted more.

Teflon got fed up, quit his job, and found his spot in the game.

He wanted to know what fast money was like. He ran into a drug dealer known as Good Money.

Good Money supplied all of the eastern district of Michigan, the northern district of Georgia, the middle district of Florida, the district of South Carolina, the middle district of Missouri, and the district of California When he met Teflon.

Right away, Teflon got close to him.

They met at a Jamaican bar and grill located off Business Fourteenth, south of Myrtle Beach.

Good Money studied the Rastafarian religion and loved to throw get-togethers in the hoods where he got his money, until one day, he met his end.

Someone kidnapped him, blew his head off, and then carved his heart out just to be sure he was really dead.

Teflon later took charge with the little he knew about Good Money's drug empire.

He started franchising numbers of companies and began to support his mother and father in addition to his own family.

After his baby mother, he never gave his heart to another woman.

Every month, he dropped large amounts of money off with his mother and father to be sure they wouldn't have to lift a finger to work ever again.

He found out later that there was no amount of money in the world large enough to stop his parents from working.

They were old school; they believed one should get a job and work.

They knew he was big-time in the drug game, but Teflon never put his fast life with family life.

When he went to clubs, he always went out of town somewhere where no one knew anything about him. He felt safe that way.

He always remembered what Good Money had taught him.

"Teflon never fucked with hotheads." Good Money had said,

"Always deal with the ones that have a lot to lose.

'Cause the ones that have a lot to lose are smarter and very cautious about their shit."

Teflon was determined to live by that rule if possible. He'd die by it.

Cristal was home in her Carrie Amber lingerie, bobbing her head to P-Money's Thunderstorm on 97.3, when she got a text from her girl Inez.

Inez wanted Cristal to give her a call when she wasn't busy.

They'd grown up together in the same hood and were the best of friends.

Inez had gone to Atlanta and gotten her cosmetology license right after they graduated from Socastee High School.

She was the type of girl who loved drama.

Cristal dialed Inez's cell phone number so they could gossip.

"Inez, what is good, girl?" she asked with her ear pressed to her phone.

"Girl, you're not going to believe what I got to tell you about your friend!" Inez screamed.

"My friend? Bitch, who are you talking about now?" Cristal asked confusingly.

Inez laughed before she spilled the latest rumor floating around in the streets.

"I heard Sunshine was at the G-Spot last night, in the VIP area sucking dicks of some nigga named Nino and his boy Rambo."

Cristal couldn't believe what her girl Inez had just told her. She sucked her teeth.

"Girl, no lie. Someone caught it, and they have it on YouTube." Inez busted out laughing.

She couldn't hold it in any longer.

"Girl, are you serious? 'Cause I'm about to go online and see this shit."

Cristal ran to her computer so she could witness what she'd just heard about Sunshine.

"Oh shit!" Cristal screamed with disbelief, shaking her head.

"Inez, look at that slut. Do she even know that she's being recorded?"

"No, 'cause they said that Sunshine was too drunk and high off ecstasy that night."

Cristal and Sunshine never had gotten along because Cristal had been told that Sunshine used to fuck her man.

Deep down inside, she'd known that C.O was seeing Sunshine on the side.

She just hadn't been able to prove it.

Cristal hated that the two of them had worked so well together to keep their little fling so low key.

"Inez, did you see the part when some dude put his hand all up in her coochie? Oh, hell no.

That is too damn nasty."

Cristal balled her face up in a disgusted expression.

And this the bitch Corey wants to fuck. Cristal asked herself,

"I'm surprised he didn't stick his dick in there." Cristal made jokes about Sunshine.

"Fuck all that. What's the business with you and Walt Diznee?" Inez said.

Cristal frowned. She didn't know a Walt Diznee. "Me and who?"

Inez knew she had a lot to catch her girl up on. "Don't act like you don't know who I'm talking about," Inez joked.

"Walt Diznee? Inez, I do not know who you talking about."

Cristal waited for Inez to fill her in.

She was becoming impatient with Inez and was ready for her to get to the point.

She never had time to run the streets, just to be in other people's business, when she was dealing with issues at home.

"Girl, your baby daddy!" Inez spilled the beans to her best friend.

"So Corey is calling himself Walt Diznee now?" Cristal sucked her teeth.

"That's what I'm hearing, and I'm also hearing he's getting his money right."

Cristal couldn't put her finger on the rumors she was hearing about her baby daddy,

"I don't know about this one, Inez."

She knew that ever since he was young, he'd always had his way of getting money.

He'd been small-time back then, but now her homegirl was acting as if Corey was the man in them streets.

It was impossible for Corey to be getting money, she thought.

He barely went anywhere!

"Isn't he on house arrest?"

Cristal wanted to be sure of his home detention, hoping he wasn't free to do anything.

It bothered her to feel that her son's father could meet some other woman and move on with his life.

"I don't know, Inez. I think you got your story mixed up." She was in denial.

"That's what I'm hearing, but the way it looks to me, the house arrest isn't stopping him, girl.

He has that Hot Road back on fire.

Girl, remember how the Hot Road used to be before he went to prison? Well, it's worse now."

Cristal got quiet.

It hurt her to hear the news of her baby daddy getting money from someone else, and she wanted to know who else knew about Walt Diznee being back in the game.

Hmm, so he's getting money now? she thought.

She felt it was her duty to know about his every move, and getting the information from somebody else about him made her upset.

"Cristal? Cristal? Hello?" Inez called to her twice before she got a response.

"I'm sorry, Inez. I lost reception just now."

Inez knew her best friend was lying but didn't say anything about it.

Both of them were with Sprint, and she knew Sprint had great reception.

"Well, that's good he's getting his money.

He's behind on Tahshawn's child support, and I need that money."

Cristal became angry at the thought of Walt Diznee getting money.

If he was getting money the way her friend was making it out to be, soon all types of bitches would be in his face.

"Damn, did I pinch a nerve when I brought Corey into this conversation a while ago?" Inez teased.

She knew that Cristal was still feeling her baby daddy, and if he had never gone to prison in the past, she would have still been with him.

They'd loved each other back in the day.

They'd been like Bonnie and Clyde when they were younger: people never saw one without the other.

"Bitch, you need to stop all that falseness." Inez read through the bullshit.

"You know damn well you're still feeling Corey."

Cristal blushed after Inez pulled her card.

She felt a slight jealousy when Inez mentioned her ex's name.

Right away, Cristal wanted to end the conversation with her best friend so she could call him.

She knew how to get in contact with him whenever she wanted to.

Cristal would block her number when she called him, and when he saw the restricted call, he knew it could be Cristal.

I hate when this dumbass girl calls me on fucking block, yo. "Hello?" Walt Diznee smiled.

"Corey, you know you're behind on Tahshawn's child support, right?"

She was being a pain in the ass toward him.

"Man, I know you ain't calling me on a child-support deal, Cristal!" he said with an fustrastion attitude.

This girl is trying everything to oppress my ass. I'm not going for it, though.

"Yeah, yeah, whatever. You can say whatever you feel.

Just know you're behind twelve thousand dollars on your son's child support, and you need to pay me.

I already got in touch with the caseworker, and she told me, I could have you put in jail, if you didn't pay the money."

This bitch is fucking crazy, yo.

I've done all that time in prison, and this ho threatens me with a child-support cost?

Walt Diznee could not believe what Cristal was doing.

Deep down inside, it hurt him badly to see her coming at him like that.

But there was nothing he could do about it.

"So you need to figure something out." She was blackmailing her baby daddy.

She was not in a good mood that day, and she wanted to take her frustration out on him.

Although Cristal knew she had done him wrong while he spent time in prison, she refused to admit her wrongdoings.

"Cristal, I don't owe you shit. If I pay the child support, it won't be to you.

I'll have to go to the courthouse and pay.

Who in the fuck you think you're playing with, yo?" Walt Diznee fussed at her.

"Well, you need to do something 'cause I need to get your son some new clothes and shoes to wear.

I hope you know that, Corey."

He didn't say anything.

He wanted to cuss her out, but he kept his cool and saw the bullshit she was trying to put him through.

"And where did you get the name Walt Diznee from? That is so lame, Corey," she teased.

"I got shit to do. Bye." He hung the phone up and right away started to distribute his drugs to the feins who'd been waiting on him to end his call.

"Let me get a hit, Walt Diznee. All I have is five dollars, man."

Walt Diznee accepted all money, big and small amounts.

He'd learned that it was the crackheads that made the dope dealer, and ever since then, he'd taken care of them.

I'd serve the crackheads before I'd supply the dope dealer in the game.

Hell, without the smokers, there's no dope dealer.

"I don't care how much money you have. You better be spending that shit with my ass.

I'm the only one that'll look out for y'all mothafuckas,"

Walt Diznee told the crackheads who stood around him.

"You're the only one that look out for us, man. That's why I don't mind spending my money with you."

Big Vess was the type of crackhead who was always around when shit needed to be done in the hood.

He drove people around who needed to go anywhere at any time.

All the person needed was a hit of crack or a few dollars.

"Like I said, I'm collecting all money. I have child support to pay."

When Walt Diznee were younger, his drug supplier Dirty had always told him, if you're going to make money in this game, never buy the same package twice.

Always remember, your next pack should be a bigger pack.

Therefore, if you buy the same package twice, that means you are fucking your money up.

W ALT DIZNEE STARED OUT HIS bathroom window at his beautiful grandmother.

She was sitting on the front porch, getting some of the fresh spring air she loved so much at that time of year.

Although she was in her early eighties, his grandmother still looked young.

The females in his family always looked young at an older age.

He loved his grandmother to death and wouldn't have traded her for another.

He went over to talk to her, because she was a wise old woman.

She was full of wisdom and had enough experience to manifest great judgment and deep understanding.

Every morning, his aunt Mary Ann would cook fish and grits, and then he would join his grandmother for breakfast.

Every now and again, they'd race to see who got done eating first.

Most of the time, he'd let her win their little race because he loved to see his grandmother smile.

It had been some years since they'd spent time together because he'd spent five years in prison, along with additional time on the run before he went to prison.

He wanted to make up for those lost moments while he had the chance, and as much as he hated to admit it, Walt Diznee knew she was slowly dying.

"Hi, Grandma. You okay?" He looked her in her wondering eyes.

"Hey, child, who's that, Corey?" she asked.

"Yes, ma'am," he responded in his little-boy voice. He was weak when it came to his grandmother.

"Hey, son, I know you're ready to get off that darn thing them people got around your leg."

They smiled at each other.

Out of all her grandboys, she'd always loved him the most. She never said it, but he could tell by the way she treated him.

"Yes, ma'am, I'm very ready, Grandma. Do you want me to get anything to drink for you before I sit down?"

She waved him off in a peaceful manner.

"No, child, ya aunt Mary Ann just brought me a glass of cold water a few minutes ago." He then noticed a glass of water sat on the table.

He sat studying her for a second and then thought back to when he was just a little boy running to her whenever his big cousin came down from up north for a family reunion, and picked on him.

He smiled at the memories.

"Grandma, when was the last time you talked to aunt Pat and Emma, they said anything about coming back home for the summer?"

He wanted to find a reason to start a conversation with her, and talking about the family was one of the best ways to get her to talk.

"Son, I talked to your aunt Pat and Emma the week before last. Hopefully they'll be coming back home.

Did you see your uncle Tom Jr. before you came over here?

I need him to cut those bushes down.

I'm so tired of seeing that darn tree every single day I come to sit on this porch."

It hurt him to notice that the tree she wanted to cut down was the tree he'd grown up playing on.

"Grandma, I came from home before I came over here.

I haven't seen him. But when I do, I'll tell him."

He stared at the old tree. He remembered the day his one-armed granddaddy had beat his ass for pulling on the limbs when he was only seven or eight years old.

I'm going to miss that old tree. He smiled.

"So let me ask you something. Did you find you a job yet?" His grandma asked.

His heart began to pound. He couldn't lie to her, so he told the truth. "No, ma'am."

She just sat there not looking at him, as if her eyes were glued to something in front of her.

He tried to look for whatever she was looking at but didn't see it. Nothing was in sight.

What the hell is Grandma looking at?

"Mhmm, Lord, I tell you. Y'all young people need to stop being so lazy.

The road y'all taking is leading nowhere fast.

And don't think I don't know what you doing Corey."

He felt busted!

He wanted to ask her what she meant. All the crack sales he'd made in the front yard replayed in his mind.

Damn, I hope she's not talking about me selling dope.

His grandmother kept her eyes ahead of her.

"Y'all better listen. Ya granddaddy and me raised twelve heads of children with the little money we made over the years.

Corey, a job ain't going to kill you, son.

See, I'ma tell you what it is. This generation today wants the fast way out."

Walt Diznee knew his grandmother somehow was talking about him.

"I tell you what. Hmm, one day y'all gonna learn.

I'ma tell you like I tell the rest of my grandkids.

I'd rather make a slow nickel than a fast dollar any day."

He put his head down.

He felt bad for letting her down, now that he was out of prison, it was his duty to show her a better him.

Instead, he'd started to sell drugs again.

"Corey, son." His grandmother paused for a moment.

She was in deep thought, wondering why Corey's generation wanted to live that fast life.

"Going down the road you're heading, you're either going back to the penitentiary or laying in some cemetery.

Y'all want to make y'all darn head hard."

Walt Diznee felt the hairs on his forearm raise.

"Rakeem, get your tail back in this darn yard, and leave that nasty dog alone!" his grandma yelled.

Walt Diznee saw his badass cousin at a distance and laughed.

His cousin Rakeem always did dumb shit and later got fussed at about it.

"I don't know what Lissa gonna do with that bad child.

She need to drop him off to his daddy."

That li'l'-ass nigga bad as fuck, Walt Diznee thought to himself.

"Ya auntie Melissa ain't gonna be able to raise that darn chile by herself."

His grandma fussed...

The thought of going back to the penitentiary made him close his eyes for a moment.

And that was the last thing he wanted to talk about.

"Son, this family has always been the black sheep. People want to see us at the bottom.

They'll smile in our faces, and behind our backs, they'll talk mean about this family.

And I'm sick of it!"

He shook his head because he knew she was right about their family being the black sheep in the hood.

And he thought back to the statement she'd made about him going to the penitentiary or the cemetery.

Why can't making money be a part of that philosophy?

"I can't believe Young Jeezy is coming to Club Toxic this Friday. And I know that shit is going to be so fucking packed, man."

Black was excited about the upcoming event.

All he ever did was get money, club, and fuck bitches.

He was the type of dude who loved to stay low key.

He was getting money but still lived with his mother and father.

Every single day, he smoked weed to calm his nerves to keep himself from slapping his jealous baby mama.

A bitch like Erica would drive her man into cheating.

She had trust issues, and Black hated it when people went to her and told her lies about him cheating on her.

Black had tried his best to be a one-woman man for her, but it hadn't worked. Now he fucked every bad bitch in sight.

"Look, my dude, I should be off this house arrest around that time.

I'm taking five bands just to blow on some ballin' shit. You feel me?"

Walt Diznee held up his right hand to impersonate a handful of money.

His boy Black was surprised when he heard his boy talking about blowing five stacks at a Jeezy concert.

He knew Walt Diznee had gotten his money up, but damn, blowing five bands in the club just to party?

That meant Walt Diznee had some dead prez in the stash.

"Damn, bra, you doing it like that?" Black smiled.

"What the fuck you mean, nigga? Ever since I been on house arrest, I took full advantage.

I saved every fucking dime of my bread.

I had Redeyes and Grouch making moves for me out there in Strand Village while me and Kim pulled strings in the hood."

Black thought about the time Walt Diznee had only bought one gram of crack.

Now he was talking about blowing bands in the club. At first, he felt bad.

How could someone have made that much money while sitting in one spot, while he was out and about moving around with a car? Right away, he wanted to be a part of whatever Walt Diznee was doing.

He'd seen the change in Redeyes and Grouch ever since their brother had come home from prison, his little brothers had money now.

Afterward, Black came around more and more every day.

Sales would be backed up, and whenever he would look for Kim, she'd be nowhere to be found.

Kim was messing up big-time.

Black watch Walt Diznee and saw the frustration written all over his face.

He had no other choice but to ask Black to run for him.

"Yo, Walt, I'm not going to even lie, man. Before you came back home, the Hot Road been dead as fuck!

Now you got this mothafucka booming."

Walt Diznee just smiled as reality kicked in, and he gained control of his anger about Kim not being there to run his sales.

He saw his progress as well!

"Put it like this, Black: just know this shit wasn't easy.

You haven't seen shit yet, though.

Wait until I get off this house arrest. Boy, my ass is going to eat."

Moments later, Walt Diznee saw Kim walking down the street.

He called for her to come over to where he and Black were chilling.

Damn, this nigga going to cuss my black ass out.

Kim could tell Walt Diznee was upset, and she was prepared for it.

"Kim, man, where were you last night when I needed you?"

Kim noticed Black standing next to her cousin and laughing at her.

She smiled because the look on her cousin's face was priceless.

The nigga was ugly!

"Boy, I was doing so much sucking and fucking last night with Whitehead.

Hell, I thought his ass just came home from prison.

That fool wouldn't let me leave."

Kim rubbed her stomach as if Whitehead had broken his dick off inside her.

"Black, let me get a light." She reached out for Black to hand her a Newport.

He laughed at Kim, and he knew she not only had been sucking and fucking all night but also had been back on the pipe, getting high.

When she lit the Newport, she inhaled and released a large, thick blue cloud of smoke into the summer air.

Like icing on a cake, right after good sex, a fresh cigarette sealed the deal.

"Damn, Kim, are you okay?" Black asked sarcastically.

Walt Diznee's mind was already somewhere else.

He knew it was about time for him to re-up on a fresh pack, but he didn't have anyone to make that move for him.

He wasn't sure about sending Black to cop for him when he knew his connection had never seen him before.

Walt Diznee and his new connection always dealt over the phone and never in person.

If Man Man had still been alive, he would have had his dope delivered to him.

It had fucked Walt Diznee up badly when he got the call from his homeboy telling him no one could find him.

When they found him, Man Man was dead in the backseat of his Bentley, deep in the woods.

It brought tears to his eyes every time he thought about it.

Damn, first my nigga Dirty, and now you.

They saw a red car pull into the driveway.

His cousin Jeff hopped out of the backseat with his brother Grouch.

Word, that's my calling right there! Walt Diznee smiled,

Right away, he came back to his senses.

"Hey, cuzo, what's up, man?" Jeff greeted Walt Diznee with a tight hug.

"What's good, Jeff? Damn, boy, you still look the same." Walt Diznee laughed.

He'd lied to his cousin; all the crack he'd smoked had Jeff looking like he was eighty years old, when he was only forty-two.

"Boy, I'm hearing they call you Walt Diznee now." Jeff smiled with missing teeth.

"Hell yeah, that's me my dawg. But let me ask you something. Who's that driving that car?"

Walt Diznee pointed at the old off-color red car parked in the old club yard where they made sales.

"Oh, that's my boy Winston. He's cool. Why?" Jeff asked.

"Man, I need a big favor." Walt Diznee paused before continuing.

He wanted to be sure he was about to make the right move in using them to drive his brother to get more dope.

"Walt Diznee, anything for you, cuzo. What you need?"

Jeff smiled, cause he knew Walt Diznee would pay well.

"Dawg, hear me out. I'm going to need you to holla at your boy. See if he'll run you and my brother Grouch to Conway to pick this work up.

I was waiting all day, man."

"Walt Diznee, don't worry about Winston. As long as you'll look out for him, he'll do it."

Jeff's words were like music to his ears. Right away, Walt Diznee started to network.

"Jeff, I got him on that. Just be sure he drives safe. But hold on for a second.

Let me holla at Grouch real quick. And I'll let you know what it is."

Walt Diznee left Jeff talking to Kim and Black while he went into the house after his brother.

Without hesitation, Walt Diznee told Grouch what needed to be done.

"Check this out. I already holla at Jeff. I need y'all to make that move to Conway and cop that work for me.

I would send Black, but that'd be a risk on my behalf, cause my connect don't know him."

Right away, his brother disliked the idea.

"Hell nah, Walt Diznee, you don't be needing to send anybody to your connect fool."

Grouch was eating a peanut butter and jelly sandwich.

"Yeah, I know, but here's the bread.

Tell Legs if all is well, I'd be needing more."

He later handed Grouch the bag of money.

"How much is this, Walt Diznee?" Grouch lightly lifted the bag of money.

"Quarter-brick money." Walt Diznee smiled and walked away after he handed Grouch the money, then told him to be careful, and he let them be on their way to Conway.

"Call me when you get there, Grouch!"

"**S**HOWCASE, WHAT IS THE BUSINESS, my dawg?"

Walt Diznee had grown up watching Showcase and other dope dealers serve crack in his hood, shit had been a lot sweeter back then.

The Hot Road had been infested with thirty or more hustlers who ran up to cars to make their sales.

At an early age, Walt Diznee would sit in his bedroom window to watch all the drugs being sold to the feins. Twenty years later, Walt Diznee had gone from looking out his window to being the supplier.

In '91 and '92, all the coke had come from up north. That shit had been only fourteen or maybe fifteen bands per kilo. But then the South had begun to take over the drug world in the midnineties to early 2000. Florida was the place to visit if you wanted a good connection on a plug.

"What's up, Walt Diznee? I'm hearing you out here doing big things, boss man." Showcase was the hyperactive type of nigga who spoke a lot and moved with anticipation, but niggas loved being around him. He had a great personality and kept things fair when it came to business.

"Showcase, I'm just starting, my nigga, but I need you, man," Walt Diznee said.

"Anything for you. What's up?" Showcase smiled, then waited for Walt Diznee to speak.

"I just got a new package in, and the way the shit looks, it's raw as fuck."

Showcase loved the fact that Walt Diznee would call him regardless of what he needed. It showed that Walt Diznee thought about him. "So what you need me to do, my nigga?" Showcase asked.

"Dawg, I got a nine-piece of soft. Come by, and whip this shit up for me. The most I really want you to bring back is eleven ounces. You feel me? I heard this bitch Pooh can whip, but I rather fuck with you. I don't know her like that."

For years, he'd grown up knowing that Showcase was the best man to contact whenever it came to cooking dope, and with some of the best coke, Walt Diznee wanted the best cooker.

"Fuck that, Walt Diznee. I'm on the way right now, and I know some people that's looking for some hard right now. Once I'm done cooking, I'll help you get rid of that shit."

Walt Diznee loved the sound of that. He was ready to get down to business. "Showcase, hurry up my dawg. How long will it take you to get here, yo?" He waited for Showcase to answer.

"I'll be there in fifteen minutes." Showcase was already heading out the door of his Landmark condo suite located on the south side of Myrtle Beach Boulevard.

"Ey, yo, Showcase, bring some baking soda before you get here." He hung the phone up and pulled the big bag of cocaine out of the shoebox by the nightstand in the room. Before he unwrapped the bag, the strong scent of pure cocaine hit his nose. A smile came across his face at the thought of his major flip. He knew he had to put up with more days and nights of house arrest before he could really say he had made it.

Selling drugs was a risk, but that was the life he'd chosen in order to get the life he'd lost back, after being sent to prison. Then a sudden rush of pain hit him. "Cristal," he mumbled, and he grabbed at his chest.

Before the painful thought of his baby mother being with someone else antagonized him, he heard a car pull into his yard.

Who the fuck is that? Walt Diznee wondered.

He hurried up to put the box of cocaine back into the shoebox and went to the door to see who was there.

There was an all-white box Chevy on twenty-six-inch Specchios. He walked to the car to see who was sitting in his yard. Before he could reach up and tap on the tinted window, it rolled down, releasing thick clouds of weed smoke. His boy Showcase stuck his head out the window and smiled. "What's up, boss man?"

They both smiled and gave each other a hard dab from the excitement of seeing each other.

"Damn, Showcase, I like this Chevy, my dawg. I might have to buy me one. This Chevy is hard as fuck!"

"Walt Diznee, I tried calling you just a minute ago before I pulled in your yard. I didn't know where you wanted me to park."

Walt Diznee scrunched up his face at his homeboy. "Damn, my bad. My BlackBerry must be on silent because I didn't hear it ring. You're good, though. Fuck it. Park here. You got the baking soda, right?"

"Yeah, I got that and my Pyrex pot." After Showcase presented all the materials, they went into the house and started to whip.

First, Showcase only cooked an ounce to see what the cocaine was about. He dropped seven grams of cut into an ounce and then added water before he placed the Pyrex pot into the microwave.

They watched the powder begin to melt and form into oil. They pulled it out, went to the sink, and ran water over the oil until it dropped to the bottom of the pot.

He watched Showcase pour the extra water out of the pot, leaving only oil.

"Yo, Walt Diznee, grab that scale for me, and pour ten grams of baking soda on a sheet of wax paper for me."

Showcase pulled out a fork and stirred the oil while Walt Diznee poured the ten grams of baking soda into the oil.

"You think that shit is straight, Showcase?"

Walt Diznee was concerned about the coke. He had butterflies dancing in his stomach. He even passed gas from the excitement of putting his new crack on the block.

Walt Diznee sat back and watched his boy do his part in turning the cocaine into crack.

"Yo, where in the fuck did you get this coke from?" Showcase couldn't believe his eyes. He looked back and smiled. He held the Pyrex pot up, showing how fast the cocaine had rocked up. "Walt Diznee, this mothafucking cocaine is off the chain. I can stretch that nine piece more than eleven ounces. I'll get fourteen with no problem." Showcase paused.

"Do what you got to do, man, but I want you to understand. I don't want no weak shit."

Showcase began right away to do his part. "Be easy, boss man. I got you on this. Just make sure you look out for my ass when I get done putting this shit together."

"I got you, Showcase. Just make sure my dope keeps them feins crawling back."

COREY N. SMALLS

"Felicia, hey, baby girl, what you up to at the moment?"

Walt Diznee wanted to check up on Felicia since he hadn't talked to her or seen her in a few days. He was starting to miss her company.

"Damn, handsome, I thought you kicked my sexy ass to the curb. I haven't heard from you in a minute." She sounded concerned about her new friend. The way he talked turned her on. His voice was heavy and had an amazing accent. She felt talking to him was therapeutic and addictive.

"Nah, brown skin, it's just that I was caught up on this bullshit with my probation officer. The bitch was about to let me off house arrest today but told me she got a call last week from somebody about me selling drugs. So she's keeping me on for another week."

He was upset that he had to wait a few more days until he was finally set free. "It's all good, though, 'cause she can't keep me on past my ninety days. Which is next week. You feel me?"

She just shook her head and felt disappointed for him. Although they'd just met, Felicia wanted him free of house arrest.

"Did you know your brother is talking about buying a G4 private plane next year? He talked with his accountant this morning about it. I just hope he knows what he's doing."

Felicia showed her deep concern's.

Walt Diznee couldn't believe what he was hearing.

"That's a lot of money being spent. I don't think Teflon will do some crazy shit like that, man. One thing I do know about my brother, he's very careful."

He tried to convince her, but he didn't know that Teflon had changed over the years.

"I don't know, Walt Diznee. I think he's not being careful about buying a stupid G4 jet."

She was upset about it. She cared about Teflon because he'd come into her life and made things better for her and her daughter, Brittney. She just wanted him to be smarter.

"Felicia, you're talking about next year. By then, he'll change his mind. Trust me!"

She just sat on the other end of the line, not saying anything. She hoped Walt Diznee was right about his brother changing his mind about buying a private G4 jet. She knew it would bring the feds down on him. Teflon had done a lot for her. If not for him, she wouldn't have been where she was at. It would hurt her to see her best friend put away for a long time. She knew Teflon was a smart man when it came to the game, including the people he chose to deal with.

Lord knows I hope Mr. Teflon changes his mind.

Felicia stressed herself over the idea. She knew that everything Teflon had worked hard for would be a waste if he bought that plane.

"Felicia, it's okay. My brother probably was looking into it. Which means he isn't going to buy a fucking private jet."

Walt Diznee laughed at her.

"But if he does buy one, then hell, let the nigga enjoy life." He joked,

She knew it wouldn't be smart to spend four million dollars on a G4. That was stupid mixed with crazy.

"Hey, Walt Diznee, can I ask you a personal question. How come you don't have a shawty? I mean, you're a very handsome guy, and you shouldn't have any problem getting any female you want."

She wanted to learn more about him. And whenever they spoke to each other, he always kept his love life a secret. She had never heard him speak about his kids or being with a woman.

"Baby girl, listen. I usually don't let anybody in my personal space. But I don't think it'll be a problem putting you down. I know I don't have any problem finding a female. It's just that at the moment, I want to keep my options open. I went to prison, and the girl I was in love with broke my heart. I'm not trying to get hurt all over again, Felicia. Sometimes I feel as if bitches ain't shit. They're in love with street niggas, but the minute we get tossed in the can, they're gone and not giving a fuck about us. Bitches be on some shit like, Out of sight, out of mind."

He was keeping it real with her whether she liked it or not.

If a bitch can love me out here, then the bitch can love me in there!
He thought angrily!

"Do you see all females as bitches because of one girl's fuckup?" Felicia asked.

"Baby girl, hear me out. Let me be a bit more specific with you. I don't see all females as bitches. I'll be calling my mother one. I'll be calling my grandma, my aunts, and females in my family a bitches."

He smiled.

"Only the ones that think they have all the senses. Thinking they can run over a nigga and get on with their life, leaving a nigga all fucked up. And I'm speaking for all the real niggas I left behind in the system. There's a lot of real niggas in the pen that had a bitch jump ship on them."

He felt angry about what his baby mother had done to him.

"Well, how do you see me? I mean, like the other day, it seemed as if you were spitting your best game to get my number."

He got quiet for a second. He couldn't believe their conversation had led up to that point.

"Felicia, look, I'm feeling you a lot. But I want to keep my options open. I'm not trying to sound like a player or anything, 'cause I'm not. It's just that I'm doing things that could put me back behind bars. And one thing I've learned is that, being in love and being in the streets don't mix. You feel me? You have to understand. I've learned the hard way."

She thought back to the time when she'd gotten hurt by her exboyfriend when she caught him and her best friend fucking in her house. She'd felt betrayed and found it hard to trust again. Felicia had tried dating afterward but never found the man she wanted to settle down with.

"Look I've been hurt in my past too. So to be honest, I can agree with you."

"That's what's up, 'cause right now, I need you to understand me, Felicia."

She closed her teary eyes and imagined what life would be like, with someone like Walt Diznee if he wasn't in the game.

"Hey, baby, can I ask you something else? When are you getting off that house arrest?"

"I'll be off Friday coming, Felicia. I thought I told you that earlier?" He sounded frustrated

"Get a room for that day. I want to give you some pussy." She smiled.

"Baby girl, you ain't saying nothing. I just hope you can take a lot of dick."

He spoke aggressively while gripping himself.

"I hope you can take a lot of pussy." Felicia rubbed her swollen nipples, which poked through her shirt.

This bitch got my dick hard as fuck!

Walt Diznee had been home for three months and not once felt a piece of pussy. The only thing that stayed on his mind was getting money and getting back on top.

COREY N. SMALLS

WALT DIZNEE SAT IN HIS PROBATION officer's office, waiting for her to return with his drug test results. He'd drunk a lot of water the minute he got up that morning, so failing the test was the least of his worries.

Being in her office made him feel uneasy. The smell and look of her office made him want to get up and leave.

The sound of other probation officers walking by, made his hands sweat. The sound of the copy machine and the rattling of keys made his heart pound and his stomach turn.

Although he wasn't in trouble, being in that environment made him nervous every time. But he needed to lighten up all the chances of his probation officer suspecting him of selling drugs.

So he'd found a pair of old boots his father worked in and had worn old, tight blue jeans with a wrinkled, dirty shirt he'd found in the laundry closet. He'd cut his cell phone off so it wouldn't ring like a lottery bell in a Las Vegas casino while he waited in her office as well.

He even thought of his brother Teflon buying a private jet next year. "That nigga is paid!", he whispered to himself.

He knew now that Teflon was worth millions of dollars. However, his feeling of jealousy wasn't as strong, as his worries about the feds picking his brother up on tax-evasion charges.

He was startled by the sound of his probation officer's voice in the hallway, and she entered the office where he impatiently waited.

"Mr. Gary, I see you're not on any type of drugs. Do you have a job yet?" His probation officer waited for him to give her an answer.

"No, ma'am, I don't have a job." His stomach turned after he responded to her.

"You've been home for three months now, and you're still unemployed?" She was disappointed in him.

"Ms. Singleton, I have my reasons." He took a deep breath.

"You have your reasons? Well, let me hear them, and it better be some good damn reasons," Ms. Singleton said.

"I went to about seven to nine different job sites and put in applications to be hired. When I fill out the application, it'll ask if I ever finished school, I'll put no.

Then it'll ask if I ever went to college, and I'll say no. Then it'll ask if I ever went to prison, and if so, when and why? So I'll put yes and then the reasons: for distribution of cocaine, possession of crack, resisting arrest, probation violation, failure to stop for a blue light, driving under suspension, trafficking, pointing and presenting firearms, simple possession of marijuana, malicious injury to personal property, simple assault and battery, and reckless driving."

While he was naming all the charges to her, she knew he was lying to her about looking for a job, but she knew she couldn't prove him wrong if he did go around filling out applications, and with a bad criminal record such as his, she knew he wouldn't have any chance of getting hired.

She wanted to throw her pen at him because he'd outsmarted her. She just sat there and stared at him once he finished.

Walt Diznee got quiet and waited for her to speak. When she didn't, he continued.

"Ms. Singleton, at the moment, I'm working under the table with Two Brothers Construction and Concrete, doing labor. That's how I'm able to pay you," he lied.

"Mr. Gary, I want you to know that I have received another phone call stating you're back out there selling drugs in the Murrells Inlet Community. And I'm also hearing you're the cause of the traffic being bad for those who live there. Do you have an explanation?" Ms. Singleton rolled her eyes at him.

"I do not sell drugs. And that's all I have to say."

He was upset about what she told him every time he had a visit with her.

This bitch could be lying. He thought.

She didn't have any reason not to believe a word he said. She reached into her drawer, grabbed her wire cutters, and then walked around to where he was sitting. She bent down to cut the ankle monitor from around his leg. For the first time in years, Walt Diznee felt free.

Hell yeah! It's on now!

He knew there were a lot of things he needed to do. When he left her office, right away, he turned his cell phone back on and checked his voice mail, and to his surprise, he only had five voice mail messages.

When he got in the car, he told his brother Grouch to spark the blunt of Kush. "Yo, check this shit out, man. Can y'all believe for the second time, someone called up here and told my probation officer that I'm back in the game?"

Redeyes was in the backseat, on the phone with one of his bitches. He told her to call back when he heard his brother's news. "Walt Diznee, say word?" He couldn't believe someone out there was trying to throw their brother under the bus.

"Redeyes, I'm dead real about that, man. Damn, there's some haters out here. It's cool, though, 'cause she still took me off that fucking monitor," Walt Diznee bragged.

"Redeyes, we got to take Walt Diznee to that new club on the beach called Plush. You know he didn't get no pussy since he came home," Grouch teased.

"Fuck y'all, and don't worry about me. I'll be getting some pussy tonight without y'all's mothafucking help! As a matter of fact, y'all need to take me to the Best Western on Twenty-Sixth Avenue on the north side. I want to cop me a penthouse for two weeks. Word! I got this bitch I wanna fuck."

After leaving Georgetown, they headed down 17 Business to Myrtle Beach. Horry County was one of the biggest counties in the state of South Carolina, a place where one could come for vacation, leave on probation, and come back for violation.

All that afternoon, Walt Diznee and his brothers rolled around Myrtle Beach. They stopped by hoods to check on the blocks they'd soon be running.

It was summertime, and people were everywhere. Small-time dope hustlers went back and forth to cars to make ends meet. Half-naked women walked the block, smoking weed and dancing to loud music that came from a Benz with the Lambo doors propped open.

Walt Diznee could tell by the look of things going on in the hood that he wanted to be a part of it.

"Hell yeah, I'm feeling this, baby." He spoke while rubbing his hands together as if he were the boss, he was soon to be.

Racepath was one of the big money spots in Myrtle Beach, and it reminded him of the Hot Road. It had its own rules. What went on in the path stayed in the path.

Not many niggas could come into that part of the city and just get money. You had to know somebody who knew somebody. The thought of it all made Walt Diznee shake his head and smile.

Racepath was his second home, cause they had family there, he was kin to the spivey family, and the rules didn't move him.

As kids, they'd spent many weekends with their grandmother Liz. And they all loved their grandmother more than anything in the world. She was well respected in the hood. Older and younger people looked up to her. She had driven a cab for many years, until she gave that life up and became a maid in the local hotels.

They pulled onto Granny Lane, and Walt Diznee's younger years flashed before his eyes when he saw the old trailer they'd grown up in.

Redeyes passed a blunt to him before they got out of the car. He hit it and then asked,

"Does Grandma still live here?" He coughed so hard that the weed smoke burnt his throat.

"Nah, she gave the trailer to Peaches, and she moved to Dogwood Apartments." Grouch brought Walt Diznee up to date on the family.

The minute they hit the porch, their little cousin came running for him and gave Walt Diznee a hug and a kiss. KeKe, Kadeem, and his godchild, Tineka, were all grown up now.

He couldn't believe his eyes. Peaches was inside, doing a woman hair and smoking a blunt at the same time. "Damn, Peaches, who's your little friend?"

Peaches was happy to see her little cousin again after he'd been away for so many years. "Don't ask me; ask her. She has a mouth of her own." Peaches spoke while staying focused on her client's head.

"My name is Ashley." She spoke softly to him.

Walt Diznee wanted to get her number. He liked her. "Well, my name is Walt Diznee. What's the deal with you?"

Ashley blushed. She could tell Walt Diznee was a playa, and for her own good, she kept her conversation short.

She looked sexy as hell; she reminded him of a black Chinese Lauryn Hill. "Hey, boo, where do you live?" he asked.

Ashley smiled. "Well, I'm from here, but I live on Forest Brooke Road, off Highway 501." She wanted to stare at him while he spoke to her, but she had to keep her head straight in order to have her hair done perfectly.

"I know where that's at. Do you live there alone, or do I live there with you?

I'm saying, like, I just maxed out a five-year bid. It'll be nice to have a place I can call home."

Redeyes was a little jealous because he'd tried for months to get that pussy, and the way it looked, it only took his brother seconds. In his eyes, his brother's game was wack. He tapped Grouch, and they laughed at him.

Walt Diznee felt the joke was about him, so he called his brothers outside. "Man, what the fuck y'all laughing at?" He felt embarrassed.

"Nigga, we laughing at your wack ass game. Walt Diznee, man, you need to stay the fuck out of prison, coming at a bitch like that," Grouch said.

"Man, fuck you. Y'all niggas is mad. That's all. As a matter of fact, let's go, 'cause Felicia is on the way down here."

On the way out, Grouch and Redeyes stopped by the trap spot to drop word to their homeboys Dex, Cheese, Jamacia and Chico about the work they had. They all agreed to start doing business together soon.

Walt Diznee just copped a brick, but he felt soon he'd be needing more. He felt a bit intense that his brother Teflon was not fucking with him, but he was out to find his own major connection and come up from there.

WALT DIZNEE SPENT MOST OF HIS night in the penthouse with Felicia. He went all out for her. He went to the flower shop and paid a florist to decorate his penthouse with rose petals and candles, big ones and little ones.

The sight took her breath away when she stepped through the door. She noticed bottles of sparkling white champagne and lobster tail with baked potatoes and a side dish of fresh salad.

Afterward, he took Felicia to the large garden tub, which was surrounded by scented candles. He kissed her while helping her undress. She went to the tub and sat in the warm water.

This nigga really don't know what he's getting himself into, doing this to me. She smiled.

"Don't move, beautiful lady. I'll be back very soon for you." He left the room, grabbed two gallons of milk, and then poured the milk into the bath water.

She enjoyed the moment and was pleased. "This is so romantic, daddy."

Walt Diznee began to sponge her off lightly. Her nipples were fully erect for him. He placed his soft tongue on her nipple and slowly sucked his way to her neck. He kissed her while his hand was under the water, massaging her clit.

She couldn't take it anymore. "Walt Diznee, please fuck me," she whispered into his ear.

But he remained cool and watched her suffer from her desperate sexual needs. He wanted to drive her out of her mind.

He grabbed her hands to help her out of the milk bath. Then he led her to the king-size bed, which had rose petals spread all over the white sheets. Felicia rolled in the rose petals while her body was still soaked with milk water. Rose petals stuck to her like paint.

Yeah, nigga, you loving this. I know!

She knew it turned him on. She got on all fours and spread her legs open with an arch in her back. Felicia looked back over her shoulder and watched him standing there staring at her pussy.

She made her ass clap and then made each butt cheek bounce up and down using her butt muscles.

"You like this phat pussy that's between my thighs?"

She smacked her ass and then turned over onto her back with her legs spread wide.

He then walked toward her and started to eat her pussy. He made Felicia pull her legs to her chest and then licked her, moving his head in a figure-eight motion.

The sucking sounds made her pussy wetter. "Eat this pudding, nigga. Yeah, daddy, you make it feel so good." She moaned.

From her pussy to her ass, Felicia had a wet spit trail from Walt Diznee's oral sex.

Damn, this nigga got a good mouth!

After a while, she stopped and forced him onto the bed. She wanted to suck his dick. He was so high and tipsy that he couldn't control the feelings of her deep-throating. Felicia was a pro at sucking his dick. "Oh shit. Oh fuck. Felicia, baby!"

She looked him in the eyes. "Mhmm!" She caressed his balls while his dick was deep in her hot and sloppy mouth. "Mhmm." Felicia moaned again. She was in love with the taste of Walt Diznee's swollen dick. "Yeah, daddy, cum on my face." Felicia massaged the tip of his head using her hands and spit. She felt his dick grow harder by the second. "I have something to tell you, daddy." She spoke to him seductively.

Without speaking, Walt Diznee stared Felicia in the eyes. He wanted to bust a nut so bad. She lightly scraped her teeth on the tip of his swollen mushroom head, causing his body to tighten. He was losing control of himself. Right before he leaned his head back to cum for her, he heard Felicia whisper, "I work for the feds!"

Before he could react, she forced his dick back into her mouth. This time, she grabbed both his butt cheeks, forced him deeper into her throat, and held him still. He moaned out loud, and his body shivered as if he were cold.

She pushed him onto the bed and then got on top of him and fucked him uncontrollably. They fucked for hours.

When they were done, they just lay in bed quietly until they fell asleep.

He later woke to the sound of his cell phone ringing. It was his boy Black. He eased his way out of bed to answer the call. "Hello?" he whispered, trying not to wake Felicia.

"Yo, Walt Diznee, what's good, my dawg? I know it's too early in the morning, but some female came to the block about thirty minutes ago, looking for you."

Black's message confused him. "What female?" he asked while looking behind him to be sure Felicia wasn't trying to ease in on his conversation.

"I don't know, man. She left me her number and told me to give it to you and have you call her ASAP. But, dawg, hear me out: the bitch is bad as hell. She came up in a fucking Buick LaCrosse sitting on fours." He gave the number to Walt Diznee, and then they hung up.

Got damn, Black. Please stop thinking with your dick all the time, nigga.

He wanted to call right away but held off until daybreak. When he returned to bed, he found Felicia playing with her pussy. She spread her legs for him so he could take a good look at it. "Hey, baby, you want some more of this wet pussy?"

He grabbed his already hard dick and climbed on top of her. He slowly eased himself into her wetness and fucked her into a deep climax.

Walt Diznee was on his way to pick his son up from his grandmother's house because Cristal didn't want him to know where her apartment was. It made him upset at times that they dealt with each other and their son through her mother.

I'm tired of this country-ass girl putting her mother in our business. She always has her mother in the picture.

Thinking about Cristal and the stupid things she did made him speed on the highway.

Felicia had gotten him a rental that morning before she headed to North Carolina. Now he could make major moves without waiting for someone else to take him places.

Hell yeah. Fuck waiting on the next man.

He called the number his boy Black had given him to see what was up with ole girl. He wanted to know who she was and why she was out looking for him.

She told him to meet up with her at the Starbucks coffee shop located in Coastal Grand Mall after he picked his son up.

"I can do that, Ms. Lady. I'll meet you there in less than an hour," Walt Diznee told the unknown female.

When he got to the coffee shop, he grabbed his cell phone to call her, and he heard a cell phone ring. Right away, his eyes followed his hearing.

That must be her?, he thought to himself.

She was sitting down, reading a *King* magazine with a mint mocha chip in her hand. He was surprised. She looked sexy as hell.

Who in the fuck is this chick, and who sent her?

He'd never seen her a day in his life. It was time to pick her mind. He didn't want her to waste any of his time, 'cause time meant money.

"Hi, Cotton Candy, and how you doing?" he said to the stranger.

"I'm doing fine, Walt Diznee. Thanks for asking." She called his name as if she knew him from childhood years.

"Oh my gosh! Your li'l' boy looks just like you. He's so cute."

Tahshawn blushed at the woman that told him he was cute.

"What's his name?" the stranger asked.

"His name is Tahshawn."

Walt Diznee got quiet. He began reading her. "May I ask you something? What's your name, and who sent you?"

He waited for her to speak while he stared into her eyes. He wanted to make her feel uncomfortable.

"I'm sorry, Walt Diznee. My name is Keya, and I came from Atlanta, looking for you. I know it may be strange to you, 'cause I don't know you, and you don't know me, but I'm going to say a name."

Walt Diznee waited for the name.

What type of game is this bitch playing, yo?

"Bandit." Keya waited for his response.

"Bandit?" He repeated confusingly. He was lost and wanted to know what the deal was with this crazy female.

"Look, Walt Diznee. Bandit sent me looking for you. He heard you got out of prison. He said y'all done time together a while back, when you was locked up in Georgetown County Jail." She stopped talking when she noticed the waitress walking by.

"Oh shit, you talking about Big-Eye Bandit."

She laughed because it was true that Bandit had big eyes.

"Okay, so that fool is in the A?" Walt Diznee smiled.

"Yeah, he told me y'all had big plans together when the both of y'all got out. So happens he made it home years before you did," she told him.

"Okay, Keya, you found me. Now what?"

She took a sip of her hot drink and wiped her mouth with a napkin.

"Hold up. Hold the fuck up! Why would he send you all the way down to the beach from Atlanta, to only to tell me this? I don't understand." He looked over at Tahshawn and noticed he was listening to their conversation, when he should've been sipping hot chocolate.

"He wants to be sure the message gets to you."

"Make sure you get the message to me? Damn, it's that serious?" Walt Diznee asked.

She looked around and then said, "Yeah, it's that serious."

He wanted to know what all this was about. Instead of just up and leaving, he ordered his son another hot chocolate and then ordered himself a chocolate mocha with a chocolate sponge cake.

He'd always loved chocolate, but if he'd been given the choice between chocolate and money, money would have been the grand winner.

He was out to get what he'd lost from doing five years in prison, and a trip to Atlanta was a move he'd been waiting for.

But what if things weren't really what it seems, and what if Keya wasn't telling him everything.

Why do I have to go to Atlanta? This nigga coulda come to me.

It was late as hell when they reached East Point, near Atlanta. Walt Diznee couldn't believe his eyes. Atlanta was new to him. The women there were about class and looked independent. In Atlanta, they lived in the latest fashion. They drove big cars—Audi Spyders, Jaguars, and Bentley Mulsannes—with the price tags still on the windows.

He knew a lot of bitches were fucking big-time drug dealers, and at the same time, a lot of them were very successful. Atlanta had a lot of opportunities for the black culture, giving them the chance to become somebody.

It blew his mind when they entered a residential area with big houses and nice cars parked out in the driveways. They pulled up into a three-car garage, and he found himself sitting next to a black-on-black Maserati GranCabrio.

They stepped into the house and entered a long, dark hallway with a large built-in fish tank running the length of the hall. It looked like the bottom of the Pacific Ocean, with pretty, exotic fishes.

Keya took Walt Diznee into an office, where he heard a familiar voice. He couldn't believe he was standing in his homeboy's spot. He looked around the office to get a better idea of his surroundings before speaking.

"Damn, nigga, are you surprised at the way I'm living, muthafucka?"

Walt Diznee couldn't believe his boy was doing so well.

"I told you it was on when I touched down." Bandit smiled.

They hugged each other. It had been a long time since they'd seen each another.

They both had been at their lowest point in life, doing a state bid, when they'd met. No one would send them money, letters, or pictures. They'd lived off the land, selling onions and bell peppers to those who always cooked jack mackerel setups. They would sell a pound of sugar and a block of butter for one dollar and then turn around and do one-for-twos on canteen items to double their profits. The penitentiary hustle had brought them together, and it had kept them close. Bandit felt that his boy Walt Diznee was the best cell buddy he'd ever had.

They sat down at the desk, and Bandit motioned for Keya to leave the room. They needed some alone time.

"So, my man Walt Diznee, what have you been up to, yo?" Bandit looked him in the face and noticed that the razor bumps on his neck no longer existed. They had cleared up well. Walt Diznee looked ten times younger now.

"Nigga, you already know what time it is with me. I'm trying to get this money right and put myself back at the top."

Bandit just shook his head and smiled. "Man, come over here, and give me another hug, man. I'm happy to see my old cell buddy out in the world." Bandit got up from his office chair to embrace him.

"Man, fuck you! Leave that cell-buddy shit behind the wall. I'm not trying to think about Evans no more, man." Walt Diznee wasn't in the mood to think about prison. He wanted money.

"Yeah, you right. You right, my nigga. Well, let's get back to why I sent my bitch to Myrtle Beach looking for your ass."

Walt Diznee smiled. "Yeah, let's talk about that. Nigga, you can't just up and send any kind of mothafuckas looking for me." Walt Diznee stopped smiling.

"Man, you good. Stop being so fucking paranoid," Bandit teased.

Walt Diznee didn't say anything; he waited for Bandit to continue.

"Walt Diznee, I want to help you, my dawg. Nigga, I'm good with that work down here. When I got out of prison, my cousin plugged me in with this connect a while back before he got hit by the feds. I'm getting bricks dirt cheap. I want to show love and take you to my man. I don't know how he'll take it. So I just rather you deal with me until then."

Bandit was a solid type of person. Although he sniffed coke a lot, he was the type of nigga who kept his business in line. He never had cared to deal with niggas who were in the game. He kept only females around. Bitches were loyal. They'd never play the game fucked up.

"Damn, my dawg, that's some real shit right there. I just copped a brick, but I could use the extra help. I got some hungry hustlers on the beach as we speak. But they're only playing with four to five ounces a day. But that shit can change with the right amount of dope."

Bandit smiled. "Listen, Walt Diznee. We got to take a ride. I got everything ready for you. I don't like keeping shit where I rest at."

Walt Diznee stood up fast from his chair. "Well, let's ride, nigga."

They went out to Strokers, where Bandit knew the owner well. They ordered Ace of Spades champagne and requested their own private dancers.

Walt Diznee loved Stephanie; she had curves no man or woman could have turned down. He couldn't believe he was up and personal with *Don Diva* Sticky Page models. They smelled good, and the way they performed in their stilettos blew his mind.

He was ready to get that bread right. He wanted to live the way his boy Bandit was living, and now he wanted to see what Bandit had for him. Walt Diznee then noticed Bandit was off in the corner, talking to one of the other strippers.

That nigga hell!

He smiled as he watched the moves unfold.

The stripper left and, moments later, returned with a Louis Vuitton duffel bag. Together, the unknown female and Bandit walked towards him.

"Walt Diznee, I hope you can handle all this work. I'm not taxing you much. Only twenty a brick."

Bandit motioned for the unknown female to hand over the duffel bag.

"That's cool, but how much is in the bag?" Walt Diznee asked.

"Seven bricks, and once you show me you can move this, it'll be more. Every now and again, the price will change. That depends on how I'm getting it."

Bandit wanted his boy to get back right. He had mad love for him, and when he'd seen how bad Cristal played him while he was in prison, he'd wanted to put him down with his sister, but Walt Diznee had declined.

"I got you, my dawg." Walt Diznee held the bag of dope tightly within his grip.

"Walt Diznee, I need you to hear me out on this. You know I fuck with you. I wouldn't do anything to shit on you. So please don't shit on me." He looked Walt Diznee in the eyes.

"Bandit, you never gave me any reason to shit on you. So why would you feel that way about me? Mothafucka, we bid together, helding each other down when no one else cared. Why doubt a nigga now?"

Bandit didn't speak a word.

"Why would you get me to come all the way to Atlanta if you're going to feel this way?"

He felt disappointed with Bandit, and if he hadn't needed the help to get his money right, he'd have left the bag of dope right where they stood and walked away. "Fool, you making me feel as if I only kept shit real because I was in prison, and it shouldn't be that way my nigga. I fuck with you,"

Walt Diznee said angrily.

"Look my dawg, behind those walls, mothafuckas have no choice but to keep it real. Once they hit the bricks, niggas are not the same. It's all about a changing face."

Walt Diznee reached over and gave Bandit a handshake. "My nigga, you have nothing to worry about."

He wanted to show Bandit nothing would ever change between them. They grabbed their bottles of champagne and toasted to the good life.

10

WALT DIZNEE CAME BACK TO Myrtle Beac the next morning with two things on his mind: Keya and how beautiful she were the first time he saw her. She was a beautiful, slim black female who'd grown up in Myrtle Beach, South Carolina. She'd moved to Atlanta two years ago and went to Emory University for performing arts.

He knew it wouldn't be fair to push up on Keya, because he knew she worshipped the ground Bandit walked on, and it could cause a lot of problems between them in business, so he forced his mind to focus on recompressing seven bricks of cocaine, not including the one brick of coke he'd had before heading to Atlanta.

He got in touch with his boy Que the minute he saw the Welcome to Myrtle Beach sign.

Que had been in the game since the age of fourteen and knew a lot of niggas who were buying and flipping bricks.

Walt Diznee had plans to be back in Atlanta before the week was out for another duffel bag.

After he found out his boy Que still had his compressor, they went into his stepdaddy's fish market and recompressed ten bricks. He left five bricks with Que and split five between his two younger brothers. He'd always felt it would be crazy to be both the supplier and the hustler. He didn't feel the need to be greedy after his boy Bandit dropped seven bricks into his hands.

Being the dealer was a lot easier for him. He only had to pick up and drop off. It made him feel good to know he had ten bricks out in the streets. He wanted to control Horry County when it came to the streets. He wanted to be the mayor. The thought of getting money made his head sweat.

He treated himself out to eat at Red Lobster, where he ordered sautéed jumbo shrimp and scampi savoiarda with a bottle of Icehouse. He was lost in his own world, until he heard his cell phone ring. He knew it was his son's mother, because every time she called, her number would show restricted. He pressed the end button so it'd go to voice mail, and minutes later, she called back.

He then began to playing mind games with her, until he realized she could be calling about their son, Tahshawn. So he answered, "Hey, what's up?" His mouth were stuffed with juicy and delicious flavored sautéed shrimp.

"Don't hey, what's up me. What's this I'm hearing you got a penthouse somewhere out here on the beach, for two damn weeks?

Then I'm hearing you went to a flower shop and paid them to decorate that shit for a bitch you just met. You are so stupid and desperate, Corey."

She was upset about the rumors she'd heard about her baby daddy catering to another bitch.

"Hold up, Cristal. What the fuck are you talking about, yo? I ain't never did no shit like that," He lied.

"Mothafucka, stop lying, 'cause I heard all about it!" she yelled. She were the type of baby mama that wants to prove to herself, that she still has him wrapped around fingers.

"Man, who told you some dumb shit like that?."

He could tell by the way Cristal sounded, she sounded very angry.

"Don't worry about who told me. But what's fucked up is that, I'm out here busting my ass five days a week to take care of Tahshawn, while you, on the other hand got money to spend on some nasty bitch you just met." He smiled at the thought her being angry.

It had been part of his plan for her to find out about the penthouse and the decoration he had done for Felicia.

He'd told Krystal, one of Cristal's close friends about his plans for Felicia. He knew Krystal talked too much, and she'd done what she was supposed to do, and that's telling in Cristal everything about the next bitch.

His baby mama was so busy yelling at him, that she didn't realize, he'd hung up, until she received a text that says, "LOL", with a smiley face.

A few days ago, while smoking a blunt of Kush with Krystal, he'd eased her cell phone out of her purse to get his baby mama's number. He wanted to play mind games with her because for four years and nine months, she'd played mind games with him. Every time he would ask his baby mother where she was or who she was fucking, she would lie and tell him, "No one." But now the tables had turned.

"Felicia, me and you got to talk and get some shit out in the open. Cause right at the moment, you got me fucked up with this fed shit."

Felicia felt bad about the way Walt Diznee treated her. He kept his conversation limited, and every time his cell phone rang, he'd press the end button. She felt as if he didn't trust her.

"Walt Diznee, why would your head be fucked up because of my dealings with the feds? What are you worried about?" She wiped the tears that ran down her face away with her bare hands, then wiped her hands against her pants leg.

"My fucking brother, bitch! What the hell you think?" He was so upset that he didn't realize he'd knocked over the bottle of wine he was sipping on.

"You know what, nigga? Fuck you. I don't need to tell you anything about me."

Walt Diznee pulled out a Glock 40 and placed it on the table. He refused to let anybody destroy his big brother's life. He wanted to know everything she was up to, and why she were after his brother. Even if it meant blowing a hole in her head. He wanted to prove to Teflon he could do things right, and killing someone who had him under a federal investigation could be the start.

Felicia began to cry. She didn't understand what the deal was with Walt Diznee. She wished she had never put herself in that position. The only way out was to tell him everything. She had never had a gun pointed at her head, and the feeling made her piss her pants.

"Walt Diznee, please don't kill me." She wiped the tears from her face.

"But before I met Teflon, I was in the streets, selling pussy, and working in the strip clubs. I needed money to help take care of me and my daughter. So running the streets was my only way to make ends meet. It was hard for me. I was in college at Horry-Georgetown

Tech, but I was so far behind on my student loan, that I had to drop out and try to find ways to pay my student loan off. And I couldn't."

Felicia wiped her tears away again. She feared for her life and didn't know what this nigga had on his mind. *Dear God, please help me!* She prayed.

"Hold up, Felicia. What the hell, all that shit has to do with my fucking brother?"

He squeezed the butt of his gun with a tight grip.

Felicia closed her eyes and breathed before she spoke. "Teflon came to one of the strip clubs the night I was dancing. Right after I performed, he called me over to his table but noticed I had tears running down my face. That night was hard for me. We sat down and talked because he wanted to know what was wrong. That day, DSS came and took my only daughter away from me."

She cracked a sad half smile at the horrible memory.

"After that night, he started to come around a lot more. We got close, and then, the next thing I knew. Your brother gave me the money to pay my student loan off. Told me this life wasn't for me and to go back to college." Felicia smiled.

She was grateful that Teflon had saved her life. "Well, I went and finished my last semester. My plans were to become a fashion designer, but when I got my degree, Teflon had other plans for me. He wanted me to work for the feds."

The idea made Walt Diznee's heart skip a beat. "For what?" He asked, he was confused.

"I didn't find out until later your brother was a big-time dope dealer. He wanted someone to be in with the feds. So he sent me."

Walt Diznee didn't know what to believe. "So you're telling me you're not out to set my brother up?" he asked after he lowered his gun.

"Hold the fuck up. Are you telling me you think I'm out to get Teflon? Is this why you got that fucking gun in my face?"

Walt Diznee began to feel stupid about what he was doing. He eased the gun back down and begged Felicia to forgive him.

She started to fuss, but the look on his face made her laugh. He looked dumbfounded. "Mothafucka, I saved your brother from an indictment on conspiracy to distribute five hundred kilos of cocaine. The minute I made office, my agent came to me and assigned me to your brother's case. I had six months to pull up anything and everything on Teflon.

But I asked for another six months. They gave me the extension, and afterward, I told them that your brother was legit and that not once throughout my investigation had he had any involvement with drugs. He spent most of his time at work and in church. I told them he loves kids and does a lot of community activities to keep kids focused and out of trouble." She rolled her neck at him.

"Felicia, I'm so sorry about this. Please don't tell Teflon. It's just that he's doing big things out there, and I'd hate to see him go down." He felt sick all over.

Damn, I'm fucking up!

"Walt Diznee, as long as I'm in that office, I promise Teflon will be good. The only thing that could fuck your brother up is if he goes out to buy that G4 jet," Felicia said.

"So have you told my brother about that conspiracy for five hundred bricks?"

Walt Diznee stood face-to-face with Felicia. He hoped she was telling him the truth about his brother having the conspiracy charges dropped.

"No, I didn't tell him." She spoke in a low tone.

"Why not, Felicia?" Everything she'd told him somewhat made sense, but uncertainty floated around in his mind.

"Because!" She was beginning to feel frustrated by him.

"Because what, Felicia?" Walt Diznee yelled.

"Because I didn't want your brother to panic and do anything stupid. I destroyed all the indictments and removed his record from the file. So what's the use of telling him for?" She rolled her eyes at him.

"How long ago was that?"

This nigga is so annoying, man. Damn.

"Nigga, that was damn near two years ago. So let it go."

I wish I'd never told you that I work with the feds, she thought to herself.

"This is what I'm thinking. If you cleared my brother from indictment charges he didn't know existed for conspiracy of five hundred bricks of coke, I have mad love for you for that.

So what happened to the mothafuckas that tried to set him up? And did you get your daughter back from DSS?"

Felicia smiled at him. She'd never seen him be so overprotective, and it was starting to turn her on. "Hell yeah, thanks to your sister Tomikcia.

But the ones that tried to set your brother up no longer exist. All them snitches is pushing daisies. All twenty-five of them. Me and my friend, the one you saw with me that day you met me, murked them ourselves.

None of them knew we worked with the feds. But we knew everything about them." Felicia wiped her sweaty palms against her shirt once more.

Walt Diznee couldn't believe what she was telling him. He respected the fact that she and her friend Pooche had gone out of their way to keep his brother Teflon on the streets. He understood why she hadn't told him about the conspiracy charges. Hell, they'd taken matters into their own hands.

"What my sister got to do with you getting your daughter back?"

Felicia sucked her teeth at him for asking a dumb question he already knew the answer to. "Isn't your sister the head lady over DSS?"

She got up and walked toward him. She got down on her knees, pulled his baggy jeans down past his dick, and sucked him until she felt him get hard inside her mouth. He reached down to pull her up and then led her to the bed. He forced her into a doggy-style position, With her ass spread, he entered her and began to fuck her hard and fast.

The thought of her being a federal investigator made him want her more.

"Yo, son, we're pushing ten bricks a month. The money is good, but we don't have the time to enjoy the wealth. We got niggas robbing the trap spot, so now Walt Diznee want us to shut down the shop that's on White Street and move business over on Warren Street. To be honest, I think that'll be crazy. Why not just get more soldiers in line?" Cheese said, not wanting to relocate from one trap to the next. It'd show no sign of weakness to Walt Diznee and his team if they stayed. "Black, to be honest, I don't think that'll be smart. The block he wants us to relocate to is being ran by some dude named Pee Wee, and to my knowledge, the nigga is doing big things over there."

Cheese tried everything in his power to convince Black so he'd try to talk things over with Walt Diznee. In reality, Cheese knew Pee Wee well. His plan was to keep Pee Wee and Walt Diznee from seeing each other. He was playing both sides.

"To be real, it is what it is, Cheese. Walt Diznee is in charge now. So if it means bloodshed, then let it be." Black, who was now part of Walt Diznee's crew, never had given a fuck about Cheese. He'd wanted to take Cheese out after he spotted him trying to holla at Grouch's wife, but Cheese had begged for Black to let him live.

"I understand what you're saying, but why go through all that bullshit? We can open shop elsewhere," Blacked said. "I'll tell you what, Cheese. Give me a few days, and let me bring this up to Walt Diznee. Maybe I can get him to change his mind," he lied.

He didn't understand why Cheese was trying so hard to keep Walt Diznee from pushing forward. Black wanted to see what Cheese was up to. He knew to keep a close eye on him and watch his every move. *Be careful, Cheese. I'm keeping you close to me for one reason and one reason only.*

They were sitting in an all-red Dodge Charger on twenty-fours. They went to every trap spot to see their progress in business and make sure things went smoothly and the feins were happy. They paid winos whatever they wanted to keep eyes on traffic. There was a wino on every block where a trap spot was located. The winos were issued Chirps, and the minute they spotted anything unusual out of the ordinary, it was their duty to Chirp security.

Ever since one of the trap spots had gotten hit by some hungry stickup kids looking for a faster way to get money, Walt Diznee had paid for extra security.

"Oh yeah, I heard about that big shoot-out you had with some nigga from Georgetown. Or was it Florence? What that shit was about, Cheese?" Black quickly changed the subject.

"Dawg, over some country-ass bitch I met at Club Isis Friday night in Pawleys Island. She came up to me, hollering at me, but the whole fucking time, the bitch's man was in the club."

Black laughed at the idea. "Man, get the fuck outta here." He knew Cheese's story had some bullshit somewhere in it, 'cause Cheese was always the aggressive type of dude who pushed himself onto a bitch. "Nigga, come on with the bullshit. I know you were the cause of that shooting that took place at Club Isis."

"Nah, Black, that's real talk. Hell, dude came up to me on some bullshit, thinking I was in for his slut. I told dude to check his bitch and not me. The next thing I know, I had to punch dude in his shit."

Black laughed—not at the incident Cheese described but at the energy Cheese put into telling lies.

While Cheese explained what had taken place that night at Club Isis, he replayed the moment by swinging his fist in the air.

"Damn, why the fuck you ain't call me, yo?" Black asked with sarcasm.

"To be honest, it would've been a waste of time. I think those niggas were trying to make a name for themselves. Them niggas had their problems with separating the difference between a goon and a fake nigga. And can you believe they followed me outside? Boy, when I pulled that trey-five-seven out—*boom, boom, boom*—cannonballs went flying everywhere."

Cheese was the type of nigga who, if you didn't watch him, would put anyone in a fucked-up position, even himself.

Not long ago, he'd met Maggie at a bike show in Atlantic Beach. She was Creole, red and thick, with icy green eyes. She was feeling him to the fullest. Maggie knew he was a dope boy, the type of man she was into.

There was something about Cheese she couldn't let go of. She had been with many dope boys but never anyone like Cheese. For the first time in her twenty-two years, she set up drug dealers from her past to be robbed. The first drug-dealer robbery they did together made her nervous. Afterward, she got used to it. It made her pussy wet.

All she knew was that Cheese turned her out. He would take her out of town to clubs where ballers hung out. He would get her to dye her hair and wear contacts to change the way she looked. They'd each enter the club alone. Her mission was to pull the type of nigga who looked like he had it. She would take him to the nearest hotel and fuck the dude until Cheese came busting in. He'd pistol-whip him and then tie him up with the sheets while she was on the bed, finger-fucking herself to get her nut.

The first night, they'd walked away with $60,000 and a half brick. Cheese was so ill that he'd had his own brother shot and killed. No one could prove he'd had it all set up, but it was strange that the car they were in got shot up without him getting hit. Right after his brother's funeral, he went to Illinois. He caught a body and then ran back to South Carolina.

The niggas he was rolling with got caught up with armed robbery, kidnapping, and possession of a firearm. Their bond got denied, but he got away in the act of a big shoot-out that left officers badly injured.

It wasn't long before Walt Diznee got put on to the heroin game. His boy Mob made a few licks out of town when he went to B-more. He heard about the business transaction that took place and waited long hours to do his part.

The minute he saw his target, he left from his hideout and went to the waiting car. There wasn't any time to waste. Mob went to the driver's side of the car, pointed a double-barreled shot gun at JuJu's head, and pulled the trigger. *Hopefully that'll be the last killing for a while*, Mob thought to himself.

He didn't shrink from it, but he disliked the complications that often came from killing. It was a messy job. When it came to the drug games, he felt all business should be run smoothly.

There was enough money for everyone, which kept a lot of people happy, but with JuJu, he was sour. Juju didn't run his business smoothly. He'd sent some bad dope to one of Mob's people, thinking he could get away with the money. Hell no! Not with Mob in the picture. Mob walked away with $300,000 and ten sealed bags of Asian heroin he took from Juju.

He kept the money but fronted Walt Diznee the heroin for a little of nothing, although he was about to see plenty of money off the large amount of heroin.

"Walt Diznee, I'm telling you, my dawg. A dope dealer needs to have a supply of everything. That goes for crack, coke, weed, pills, and heroin."

Walt Diznee couldn't believe his eyes once he opened the heroin business. One of his spots was in Burgess, on Circle Lane, and the other was on Cocoa Street. Each spot counted at least thirty sales per hour. Both were run by all bitches. Because of Mob, he found a major connection in Baltimore and had things set up to be shipped by boat from one fish market to the next.

His boy Que agreed to have the fish stuffed and shipped to his stepfather's fish market, as his stepfather was out of town for the next seven to eight days.

Once the shipment made it safely to its location, Que removed two big clear bags of China white from each fish. He spent all day unstuffing fish until his job was completed. Minutes later, Que contacted Walt Diznee.

"What's good?" Walt Diznee asked after picking up on the first ring.

"Nine." Without saying another word, Que ended his call.

Walt Diznee smiled to himself after putting his cell phone in his pocket. "Nine today. Fifteen tomorrow."

He'd make a lot of money once he planned his distribution route. His main focuses were Georgetown, Charleston, Spartanburg, and Columbia.

Each key of heroin would be cut with morphine powder.

After mixing the entire batch, they divided others into bundles and slips that could be sold in the hoods.

Having plans to move numbers kilo's of heroin a week. He was pleased with the expansion of his distribution network.

He wanted to do better business with his boy Bandit when it came to buying coke, but lately, he'd kept coming up short on the product.

He wanted to cut out the middleman and deal hands-on with the main source, but he didn't want to cut Bandit out of anything he'd started years before he came home from prison.

He just wanted Bandit to step his game up and supply him with whatever his money could buy.

Walt Diznee was in Coastal Grand Mall with his two younger brothers and their cousin Punch. They damn near shut the stores down whenever they went shopping.

They went into Dillard's, Street Stuff, Hood Goods, and more. However, a moment spoiled everything when they came out of the Lidz hat store. "What the fuck?" Walt Diznee was hurt. They all stared at the two people sitting before them. "Yo, who the fuck is that with her?"

Redeyes looked at Grouch and then shook his head.

"Y'all know who the fuck he is?" Walt Diznee asked. They both just stood there not saying a word when Walt Diznee glanced at them.

"That's Pee Wee." Punch spoke up. He knew of Pee Wee through a mutual friend.

"Pee Wee!" Walt Diznee repeated the name. Pee Wee was another big-time drug dealer on the streets of Myrtle Beach. He not only pumped drugs but also ran a prostitution service. Pee Wee had left New Orleans because he had a large price on his head. He'd gotten into a big shoot-out with another pimp because he started working his bitches on someone else's block.

Jazzy was one of the biggest pimps and heroin dealers in New Orleans, and after he was shot and killed, Pee Wee couldn't be found, so Jazzy's crew began to do drive-bys on Pee Wee's mother's house. The bullets from an AK-47 caught his younger brother in the back of his head. Right away, he left town and took his bitches with him.

"So that's who Cristal's fucking?" Walt Diznee was so hurt he didn't realize the question he'd asked. He couldn't believe his baby mother was in the mall, eating Chinese food with another man. She was really enjoying his conversation and kept a smile on her face. She looked good as hell.

There was a saying that an ex always looked better when you were not together anymore, and for the first time, he began to believe that. *Damn, this shit hurts so bad, seeing her with him.*

Grouch stood next to his brother and felt his pain. "Man, Walt Diznee, don't let that shit fuck with you." He tried to pull him in the opposite direction, but Walt Diznee refused to move.

"Listen, tonight I'm heading to Atlanta to see Bandit. I want the three of you to find out everything about that bitch-ass nigga. If y'all got to buy some work from that clown, then do that. I want to know how his dope is, how much he charges for a brick, and where he supplies everything at." Without speaking another word, he walked away, heading for the entrance of Coastal Grand Mall.

Walt Diznee couldn't believe he'd never heard of Pee Wee. And how come they hadn't bumped heads in the streets? Right now, it didn't really matter. What truly mattered to him was his family—and the streets of Myrtle Beach.

12

I T WAS EARLY SATURDAY MORNING WHEN they arrived in East Atlanta, Georgia. Seeing a lot of beautiful women was normal in the A, but every time Walt Diznee went, the sight drove him crazy. He wanted them all.

Keya, whom he'd met through Bandit, was five foot six, had smooth baby skin, and was slim, with a bubble ass. Her bottom lip was juicy. He loved the way she smiled and the way she took care of herself. She stayed on the other side of Atlanta, in Riverdale, Georgia, but that day, only one female was on his mind. He kept thinking about his baby mother.

He wanted her back, and seeing her with another man had fucked him up. He'd never felt about another woman the way he felt about Cristal. She was beautiful. Throughout his years of living, he had fucked some of the sexiest bitches who'd ever walked on the face of planet Earth, but there was something about Cristal. He couldn't get her out of his system no matter what he tried and did. *I can't believe that bitch has me hooked.* He shook his head in disgust.

They were passing through the Sun Valley complex and noticed police cars, fire trucks, and forensics people with a lab truck. Everyone was looking at two bodies lying on the ground. The victims had been shot to death. A police officer was talking to an older man, taking notes.

Walt Diznee looked in the passenger-side mirror to be sure no police cars were behind them. Then he patted his right hip to ensure that his pistol was where he'd put it.

They made it safely to their destination without being pulled over with a South Carolina tag. Although his boy Showcase had a license to drive, he wasn't in the mood to be fucked with by no cop.

"What's good, my dude? Me and my people is here. Same spot." Walt Diznee texted Bandit instead of calling. He felt things were safer that way.

"That's what it is, Walt. I'll be there in about an hour or so."

Walt Diznee rubbed his eyes. He was tired from the six-hour drive, and all he wanted was some rest. "Showcase, ole boy should be here within the next hour or so. I'm going to take a quick rest until then."

Showcase was sitting on the coffee table in the condo, flipping through the channels to find BET. "You good, my dude. What you need me to do when he gets here?" Showcase asked.

"If I'm still asleep, wake me up. 'Cause the minute he comes with the work, I want us to get back on the road."

Before he went into the next room, he received another text: "Ey, my dawg, I know you put an order for fifteen, but all I got is ten. Is that straight?" He shook his head in a disapproving manner. "As always! Showcase, read this bullshit." He handed his BlackBerry to him. "Man, that fool always pull some stunt like that on me, yo." Walt Diznee was too tired to put up a fuss about the lack of work from his boy Bandit. "You know what? As soon as I find me another connect, he's done!"

He texted Bandit back: "Just bring what you have. I got to get back on the road. Got shit to handle. Erase texts!" Walt Diznee went to the back room and lay down.

Hours later, he found himself having dreams that caused him to break out into a cold sweat. He woke up after he saw an image of his grandmother walking upstairs into heaven while looking back at him and waving. "Corey, chasing the wind is worthless!" she'd said. Walt Diznee wanted to know what she'd meant.

After wiping the sweat away from his moist face, he had noticed it had been two hours since he'd fallen asleep. He got up from the large condo bed, walked into the living room, and noticed Showcase was sleeping on the couch with the TV on.

I wonder how long this nigga has been asleep.

"Damn, nigga, get up, yo!" Walt Diznee shook him. Right before Showcase got up, he heard a knock at the door. *Damn, I hope that's Bandit.* He looked through the peephole to see who it was. It was Bandit.

"It's about time you came, mothafucka. Hell, you had us on a two-hour wait, when you told me an hour or so." It really didn't bother Walt Diznee because he'd slept the whole time, but on some real shit, the nigga thought he'd missed Bandit by an hour because he'd overslept and then woken up to find his boy Showcase passed out as well.

"Walt Diznee, let me put you down on what's going on. I knew you wanted the fifteen, so I made a few calls to some people I knew was straight. I had to go out to Decatur to pick the other five up on my face," Bandit said while handing over the duffel bag.

"So this fifteen in the bag?" Walt Diznee asked. He went into the back room, got the money, and handed it over to Bandit.

"Yeah, it's all there. I wasn't going to have you come all the way to the A and not have what you wanted. You feel me?"

Walt Diznee looked over Bandit's shoulder to get a good look at the thick, tall yellow bone standing behind him. *Damn, that bitch is right!* He glanced over at Showcase and just shook his head.

She smiled once she realized they were interested in her. She was feeling them both as well. She loved the way they talked. They didn't sound like the niggas from Atlanta, and it made her pay more attention to them. *These boys are country as hell,* she thought.

"You might have to stretch this fifteen as much as you can," Bandit said. "Shit is getting hot around Atlanta. If you paid any attention to the billboards coming into Atlanta, that shit says, 'If you think it's a drought now, wait until next month.' The fucking feds in town. If not now, hell, they will be soon, Walt Diznee."

Oh shit, I did see that sign. This fool waited until I come to Atlanta to tell me this shit? Walt Diznee thought. "Well, I think we need to get moving. Call me as soon as things get right, Bandit."

Without any hesitation, Walt Diznee and Showcase were on the road, heading back to Myrtle Beach.

Walt Diznee grabbed his cell phone and called a Benz dealership. It was a blazing-hot, humid day in his upscale gated residential neighborhood. The temperature was in the high nineties—so hot that one's nose could begin to bleed.

After looking through the *Sun* newspaper and reading the heat index, Walt Diznee right away wanted to buy himself a car just to stay out of the heat. *It's too damn hot not to have a car, yo,* he thought. He tossed the paper aside and called the number of the local Benz dealership he'd seen in the car section. *If I'm going to buy a car, hell, go all out with the shit!*

"Hello. I'm calling about the Maybach 57 Benz I saw in the ad. Yeah, that's right." Walt Diznee was about to buy himself his first new ride. Ever since he'd gotten back into the game, he'd been getting rentals. "Right now if you want. Okay, I'll be there in less than an hour. That's fine. Thank you. I'll be right there. Bye." He hung up and called Creekside Cab to take a cab to the Benz dealership.

He grabbed his Louis Vuitton roller suitcase and loaded it with the money he needed to buy the car. Fifteen minutes later, his cab was waiting outside.

Walt Diznee got dressed to show his most sophisticated appearance. His father had always told him, "Never step into a place of business looking like a thug."

Before he left, he sprayed on his favorite Dolce and Gabbana cologne. He stepped into the cab, pulling his suitcase behind him. "Where to, sir?" the cab driver asked while looking in the rearview mirror.

"Take me to Lopez Luxury Auto Sales right off Business 501, please."

It was a busy day. Tourists came to Myrtle Beach that time of year to visit the lively city in South Carolina, which made it hard for the locals to get where they had to be at a set time.

He glanced over to his left and noticed a bad car wreck on the opposite side of the main highway, in front of the factory outlet stores.

While he was in the cab, his mind drifted off to the dream he'd had of his grandmother. It bothered him a lot. The only way to get his answer was to go to his mother.

Every time she told anyone about a dream she had, it always presented itself—if not with her, then through someone else in a different form. It had gotten to the point that no one wanted to hear about Gayle's dreams. Her dreams scared everyone who knew about them.

A while back, she'd told everyone about a dream in which she was walking around four closed caskets, not knowing whom the four caskets belonged to. Like wildfire, her dream had spread among the community. A week later, four relatives on his father's side of the family had been killed in a bad car crash.

Chasin' the wind is useless? Walt Diznee kept repeating what his grandmother had told him in his dream. He couldn't understand what it meant. The thought vanished once he saw the Lopez Luxury Auto dealership.

"Thank you, sir." Walt Diznee paid the cab driver and tipped him for his good work ethic. He felt that every man had a hustle within him, and he respected the deeds of a person who activated the will to hustle. The cab fee, he knew, went to the company, but the tip went to the driver.

"Do you want me to wait, sir?" The driver put his cab in park.

"Nah, I'm good. Thanks!" Walt Diznee struggled to pull the suitcase stacked with money out of the cab.

He walked through the double glass doors and noticed a beautiful woman walking toward him. "Welcome to Lopez Luxury, sir, and how may I assist you today?"

The beautiful saleswoman looked to be in her late twenties or so. She had a petite body, a honey-tan complexion, hazel eyes, thin lips, and a dark brown beauty mark on her upper left cheek. Her hair was pinned up like a rooster tail. Walt Diznee studied her feet and toes, which were small and cute, just as he liked. *Damn, bitch, you're fine.* He was hypnotized.

"My name is Jennifer Rodriguez, and I'm the assistant manager," she said.

"I called a minute ago about the car." He spoke to her without blinking. He wanted to enjoy every moment of looking into her eyes.

"What's your name?" she asked, slightly licking her lips.

"Corey Gary, ma'am." His heart thumped with an intense heartbeat.

He felt weird. It had been a minute since he'd used his government name. For many years, he had been living under an alias. From 1994 to 2005, he'd been known as someone else. The street life had stripped him of his true identity. *Damn, it doesn't even feel right to say my real name.*

"May you wait here, please?" Jennifer Rodriguez disappeared and then came back a moment later with a male figure.

"Mr. Gary, how are you today, sir? My name is Mr. Lopez. And you're here to purchase the Benz you called about, right?" Mr. Lopez smiled. He'd reached his sales limit for the month. He'd sold ten Benzes in all.

"Yes, sir!" Walt Diznee told the happy salesman.

"Cool. Follow me, please." Mr. Lopez took him to the office and right away started the paperwork for his car purchase. "Okay, Mr. Gary, how are you willing to pay?"

Walt Diznee reached for his Louis Vuitton suitcase and unzipped it.

"Cash!" Mr. Lopez couldn't believe his eyes. "Hold on, sir. Let me have my assistant manager put up the Closed sign, and we can start business."

Seconds later, Mr. Lopez returned to his office with Jennifer Rodriguez by his side. Like every other businessman, Mr. Lopez whispered something to his assistant. They didn't know that was one of Walt Diznee's biggest pet peeves. He hated whispering. He slightly shook his head. It made him want to go elsewhere to do business, but he thought, *Fuck it. I'm here now!*

"I'm sorry, Mr. Gary, but I've just gotten a very important phone call, so I'll be leaving my assistant sales manager to take care of you, if you're pleased with that?" Mr. Lopez stood next to Jennifer Rodriguez and waited for Walt Diznee to respond. He wanted to be sure his customer was satisfied with the switch. For a man of business, Walt Diznee understood what time it was.

When it came to money and business, you had to be a multitasker and learn to be in more than one place at one time.

"Yeah, I'm cool with that, but before you leave, I really need you to understand that I need y'all to hook the paperwork up like I'm making payments. I don't need the IRS all in my shit," Walt Diznee said.

"Trust me, we've dealt with your kind before. We'll hook you up." Mr. Lopez left the store in a rush to handle other business.

"Okay, Mr. Gary, let's get this paperwork out of the way, shall we?" Jennifer Rodriguez said.

They sat and talked while completing the paperwork. It turned him on to watch her work in a sophisticated manner. He could tell she really knew what she was doing. She went through all the paperwork as if it were something she'd been born to do.

"Okay, Mr. Gary, I will need you to sign here, here, and here."

Damn, how many times I got to sign my name to buy a car? he asked himself.

She left the room and came back with the keys. "May you follow me, please?" She handed him the keys. "There's your sexy Benz."

Walt Diznee unlocked the door, got inside, and sat in the large, soft leather seat. He turned the key in the ignition, and the engine started immediately. The mileage showed zero miles on the odometer.

Jennifer Rodriguez sat down on his lap and then reached over to show him how to work the navigation system. She felt his dick getting hard and hit the seat control to slide the seat back a bit farther away from the steering wheel and turned to face him.

Yo, this bitch is a freak.

"You know what turns me on, Mr. Gary? It turns me on when a thug tries his best to cover up who he really is."

Walt Diznee was confused. He jerked his neck and tightened his face, not knowing what she was insinuating.

"Come on, nigga. I know you're a dope boy. I can tell by the way you talk, the way you dress, and most definitely the way you're spending all that money." She climbed into the backseat, revealing her pretty shaved pussy when her short business skirt eased over her ass. "Didn't you read the fine print in the ad when you saw the Benz?" Jennifer pulled a box of Magnum condoms from the console. "It states, 'If you buy this Benz, ladies will be all over you.'"

Walt Diznee grabbed the box of condoms and hopped into the backseat with her. He forced her into a doggy-style position and fucked her so hard she screamed at the top of her lungs until he came.

Walt Diznee couldn't believe what had just happened in the backseat of his new Benz. "Damn, baby girl, that pussy is right. It must've been a while since you fucked. Your pussy tight as hell." He breathed hard while lying in his backseat.

She went to the restroom, found a clean rag to wipe herself, and then went back to the Benz to wipe Walt Diznee off.

She glanced back at him while she held his dick. "Boy, this dick is too big. I can't believe you had all this in my pussy." She leaned over and gave his dick a kiss. "Oh yeah, Mr. Lopez told me to put his dealer tag on your car until yours comes in."

They traded numbers, and she sent him on his way.

He looked in the rearview mirror at himself and smiled. *Yeah, now it's time to really show these fuck-ass niggas who's running shit.*

13

THE NEXT DAY, WALT DIZNEE went to his mother's house to spend time with her.

He noticed his father were in the room watching television, when he walked through the back door.

"What's good, ole man?" He gave his daddy the peace sign as he continued to walk to the kitchen.

"You stay there and think I'm old if you want to."

Walt Diznee smiled at his daddy. Him and Teflon always called him old just to pick at him.

"As long as ya mother okay with it, that's all that matter. You and ya brother Domonick need to move them piles of wood I got stacked up on the side of the house to the shed, Corey."

"Daddy, I'll have to pay Uncle Tom Jr. to do it 'cause I'm tired, man." Walt Diznee sucked his teeth. He looked out the kitchen window and noticed his uncle Bubba outside cooking on the grill. The smell of barbecue made him hungry.

Uncle Bubba don't be playing when it comes to cooking on the grill.

He thought to himself, and knew within the next hour or so, their yard will be over flowing with hood guests.

He loved being at his mother and father's house so he could eat and rest in peace without anyone fucking with him.

It was the one place in the world where he could feel like a kid again; being bossed around by his mother, father, aunts, and uncles; and fuss back and forth with his brothers as if they were teenagers again.

"Mama, I need to ask you something."

His mother was in the kitchen, cooking fried pork chops, pork and beans, and rice. The food reminded him of his younger years before he went to prison.

He and his three brothers had grown up on that meal, but now he covered his mouth and nose whenever he was around pork. Ever since he'd become part of the Nation of Islam, he'd changed the way he ate.

"What is it, Corey? And y'all know I don't like to be bothered with while I'm cooking."

He smiled. *My mom hasn't changed a bit.*

"Okay, I had this dream yesterday about my grandmama. She was walking into heaven on some flight of stairs. But she stopped midway and looked back at me. And all of a sudden, she said that chasin' the wind was useless. What do you think she meant by that, Mama?"

He paused to hear what his mother had to say.

"Well, Corey, the only thing I can tell you is to read the Bible and put yourself back into church. Maybe that's what she's trying to tell you. 'Cause you know y'all out there selling that stuff to people, and y'all know that isn't right, Corey.

Maybe she's trying to tell you that chasin' that fast money is not good. You just came home from prison Corey, and you're back out there doing the same thing that took you away from us the first time."

He felt guilty. "Mama, man!"

She went to her bedroom and later came back with an old Bible that had Mrs. Arlene printed on the front.

"Here this Bible came from your grandmother. You need to read it. And don't 'Mama, man' me. I done told you, Corey I ain't no man."

He reached for the Bible and then rubbed his thumb across his grandmother's name. It almost brought tears to his eyes when he remembered always seeing his grandmother with it.

Chil', I'm going to tell you right now. There's only one or two things that's going to happen. That's either the penitentiary or the cemetery.

His grandmother's statement replayed in his head.

"Damn, Grandma. I hope you're wrong on this one," he whispered.

Now she was gone, and the only thing he had of her was her Bible. "Thanks, Mama."

He took his grandmother Bible his mother gave him and went to his old room and lay in bed.

He needed some time to himself. He knew the life him and his brothers were living was wrong, but the street was in them. Many thoughts came into his mind, even thoughts of his baby mother.

"What's up, baby? Is it okay if I give you a lap dance?"

She came into his room with only a bra and thong on. And walked toward him with sex in her eyes. She wanted him.

"Hell yeah, baby, come here so I can squeeze that ass."

She pushed him back onto the bed. "No, baby, no touching."

She laughed and then turned around, bending over to touch her toes, and pulled her thong to the side, showing him her pussy.

"You like that?"

She asked, then slapped herself on the ass and then began to dance, making her ass clap.

She knew it turned him on. "Go ahead, baby. Make it rain for your babymama."

Walt Diznee reached for his safe and began pulling money from it, then started to toss hundreds of dollars at her. The more he tossed money, the more she screamed, Child support! Child support! Child support!

Walt Diznee later woke to a loud knock on his bedroom door.

"Corey! Corey... get up! Somebody outside to see you, boy!" His father yelled.

Walt Diznee looked around the room. He felt his pocket and wiped his face, realizing he'd had another crazy-ass dream. "Damn, what the fuck that shit was about?" he whispered while wiping the sweat from his forehead.

He walked toward the door but looked behind himself before leaving his old room, to be sure his baby mama really wasn't there.

"I'm tripping like a mothafucka, yo." He shook his head and laughed at himself.

The minute he stepped outside, he saw Napo standing by an all-red Dodge Magnum sitting on twenty-four-inch rims. The windows were tinted so dark he couldn't see who was sitting on the passenger side.

"Look at my boy!" Napo yelled.

He was the flossing type of nigga with a big ego.

Napo blew money as if it grew on trees. A lot of niggas disliked him because he was quick to fuck their bitches. The majority of his beef came from fucking the next man's bitch, but other than that, the nigga was a cool-ass individual.

Napo's connect had gotten hit by the feds a few weeks ago, which caused him to bounce around from one dealer to the next until he found a steady supplier.

Walt Diznee walked up to Napo, and they gave each other daps. *Look at this pretty-ass nigga. Every time he steps out of the house, he's got more than three big diamond chains on.*

"Napo, what's good with your flossing ass? A mothafucka gonna rob your ass one day, flossing the way you floss, yo," Walt Diznee teased, but he had to admit the nigga was fly as hell, and if he'd had any bitches, Napo would have been the first nigga to call to roll with him.

"Fuck these niggas, man. If they come, they better come right or don't come at all."

Walt Diznee knew Napo didn't give a fuck. If he had, he wouldn't have flossed the way he did in the streets.

"Walt Diznee, what's good, man? I was trying to get in touch with you this past week. I came to your mom and daddy's spot and asked Teflon how I could find you."

Napo was stressed about not having a good connection. His money was running low because of all the other weak dope dealers he'd trusted to spend his money with had bad coke.

And now that he'd finally gotten in touch with Walt Diznee, he wanted to do business with him. He knew that by dealing with Walt Diznee, he could get his money back right, due to the good coke and heroin he supplied the street with.

"The whole time, you were knocked the fuck out." Napo patted Walt Diznee on the left shoulder.

"It's been a rough week for me, Napo. I came here to spend time with my mom and pops. I barely be around that much. I'm a busy man."

Napo saw the stressed look in Walt Diznee's eyes.

"Damn, Walt Diznee, what's good?" Napo showed his concern. Although he'd come for business, he wanted to show that he could be a friend as well.

"Shit, what's good, my dawg? You aight?" he asked again.

They just stood there looking at each other.

What the fuck is up with this dude? Walt Diznee wondered.

"Look, my dude, I know this isn't the proper time or place to holla at you, but I really needed to talk to you, my nigga. I'm hearing you're doing big things right now on that coke and heroin. You feel me? At the moment, I got Pawleys Island in the palm of my hand."

Walt Diznee just listened to what he had to say. Napo didn't know that Walt Diznee had already gotten the 411 on who ran Pawleys Island.

He already knew about Napo and the movement he had going on, on the Island. And to his surprise, he was very impressed with Napo's work.

"Bee Gambino got hit by the feds, so I'm out putting food on nigga's table now. But the work that I'm getting from the country isn't all that good. Them country niggas stepping on everything, and it's fucking my money up."

Walt Diznee knew that Napo was telling the truth; he'd heard about those country boys and how they were always stepping on the coke and then putting it back on the streets at a high cost.

"They sold a brick for twenty-five thousand, but it was cut so bad that the coke wouldn't bounce back. From thirty-six ounces to thirty-two ounces is what you'll get, man. That shit is pathetic, bra."

Napo was getting upset just talking about it. "Dawg, don't tell me them country boys are doing some crazy shit like that." Napo shook his head.

He needed help, and he knew Walt Diznee was the only person who could help him.

Every time Napo moved, his diamond chains made loud crashing sounds, and rainbow colors reflected from them.

"Real talk, Walt Diznee. I'ma kill one of them mothafuckas for playing with that work. So what's good, man? Fuck with me, yo."

Walt Diznee and Napo both turned their heads toward the direction of distant yelling and recognized the loud, raspy voice of Walt Diznee's uncle Franklin.

He was yelling at his all-black full-blooded Lab, Big Bear.

"Yeah, my dawg, I'll fuck with you. So what you trying to do?" Walt Diznee asked.

Right away, Napo rubbed his hands together as if there were lotion on them. He was ready to begin business today.

"Right now, I'm trying to cop three bricks of that Play-Doh," he said.

But before Walt Disney had the chance to respond, they saw Redeyes pull into the yard in a S400 Benz he'd bought just days after Walt Diznee copped his Maybach.

He parked but didn't got out.

Redeyes was talking on the speaker phone to one of his bitches. He loved playing mind games with them.

Walt Diznee refocused his attention on Napo. "I only have two at the moment, but hold on for a sec. Let me see what my stupid-ass brother has on him. That nigga is hot; he always drives around with work on him. If not, then I'll have to call Grouch."

While approaching the car he heard Redeyes unlock the doors for him to hop in. Right away, he spotted two twin .40-caliber Smith and Wessons lying on his lap, and in the console of his car was a P89.

"Redeyes, you have any work on you?" Walt Diznee asked.

He knew his brother had dope, 'cause his little brother never went anywhere without his guns if he had work in the car.

"Hell yeah, I got a little something. Why?" Redeyes placed both guns on the passenger-side floor beside Walt Diznee's feet.

"Napo wanna cop three bricks, but I only have two on me at the moment. You feel me?"

Redeyes glanced at Napo and laughed. He knew already, before it was all said and done, them Pawleys Island niggas would be copping work from them.

"That nigga was fucking with Bee Gambino, right?" Redeyes asked.

"I think so, but he was telling me his connect got hit by the feds. And now he wants to fuck with us."

Redeyes smiled. "Hell yeah, he been dealing with Bee Gambino until Bee Gambino got knocked by the feds."

He reached into the backseat, grabbed his Louis Vuitton duffel bag, and handed the bag to his brother.

"That's a brick right there. Tell Napo I said what's up. Tell that nigga I said he never came through with that bitch he had for me the other night." He laughed.

"I hope you know I can hear you, Redeyes." A female voice came over the surround speaker system.

Redeyes waved her off as if she were a fly. "Girl, shut up! Ey, Walt Diznee, I'm about to bounce. Put that bread in Mama's house, yo. As a matter of fact, just knock that off from what I owe you."

After Walt Diznee got out of his brother's Benz, Redeyes backed out of their yard and drove away.

Ǫ

It was a little after midnight when Felicia got out of the shower. She went toward Walt Diznee's master bedroom but noticed he wasn't there. She wanted to be sexy for her man and put on Victoria's Secret lace boy shorts with a bra that matched.

She oiled her body to give it a shine that'd help boast the curves.

She went into her night bag to get her Prada perfume, sprayed a little on the front of her boy shorts, and stood in front of a body mirror to get a better look at the body she admired so much.

She pulled her left titty out and then sucked on her nipple. It'd be a bit sexier when he saw her nipples nice and hard for him.

She then reached her hand between her thighs to rub her pussy. "Oh, Walt Diznee, yeah baby, just like that. Mmm." She moaned softly.

Felicia closed her eyes and leaned back at the good feeling she'd given herself, until she heard Walt Diznee's phone rang on the king-size bed.

Her heart jumped, causing it to beat harder. She thought he'd caught her in the act of playing with herself. She blushed.

She went over to the bed, stared at the screen display, and noticed it said, "My Boo." *Oh, hell no.*

Right away, Felicia wanted to press the talk button to find out who it was.

I know this jackass boy isn't playing me, right? she kept asking herself repeatedly.

She pressed the end button so the call would go to voice mail. Then she heard him coming up the stairs toward his master bedroom.

She wanted to throw anything her hand could grab, at him the minute she saw him come through the bedroom door.

Instead, she played things cool.

"Felicia, was my phone just ringing?" He stared at her waiting for her response.

She was staring into the two-hundred-gallon fish tank he'd paid an arm and a leg for.

"No," Felicia lied. She was angry as hell.

Walt Diznee walked toward the bed to get his phone but couldn't find it.

"Where's my fucking phone, yo?" He began tossing pillows off his bed onto the floor in search for his phone.

"Here, nigga. Your fucking phone is right here." She handed him his phone.

"What the fuck you doing with my phone anyway, Felicia?"

We're not going to begin this type of game! Fucking with my phone and shit, he thought to himself angrily.

He glanced at the screen and saw one missed call. "I thought you said my fucking phone wasn't ringing."

Felicia just kept her eyes on the large fish tank, not saying a word to him.

He'd gotten caught red-handed. *Ah man, she caught me!*

Walt Diznee headed out of the room, until he heard Felicia behind him. He tried his best not to crack a smile and kept his back turned toward her.

"Yeah, you stupid mothafucka. Why the hell you got to leave the room to call back? You pussy. I bet it's a bitch. Don't fucking play with me, boy. I ain't for that shit!" she yelled at him at the top of her lungs.

He realized that whenever she got upset and began to yell, she had an irrational, high-pitched tone of voice he couldn't stand.

"Felicia, what the fuck is you talking about? Look, I don't have time for this bullshit today. Fo real, yo!"

They yelled back and forth.

"You damn right, nigga! I'm that bitch! I'm that Ms. Bitch too, with your weak-ass dick. Who in the fuck is 'My Boo' you have programed in your fucking phone?"

He turned his back on her once again. He didn't want to bust out laughing in her face. He was caught as sure as shit.

Damn, I'm slipping. You'sa stupid-ass nigga for this one, Walt.

"Yeah, nigga, tell me. Who's that bitch? Yeah, mothafucka, I saw your phone. I should've answered that shit with your sloppy ass."

He tried to walk away from her, but Felicia wouldn't let him. "That's your fucking problem right there, Felicia. If you wasn't so damn nosy, we could've been fucking instead of fussing over dumb shit."

He tried his best to find reasons for having another female's number in his phone.

He knew Felicia was a good person at heart, but he wasn't ready to settle down with her. His heart was still with his son's mother, but he didn't have the courage to tell her that much.

"Nigga, please. You ain't getting none of this pussy. Go to that bitch you got as your boo in your phone."

Once again, his phone began to ring.

"Go ahead, mothafucka. Answer that shit. Answer it, bitch. So I can slap your ass." She kept pulling on him as he tried to get away.

Damn, I hope this isn't Keya, he thought.

Ever since Walt Diznee and Bandit had stopped doing business, him and Keya had started fucking around on the side behind his back. Nothing serious—only friends with benefits.

Every time he turned to sneak a peek at his phone to see who was calling, Felicia made it hard by trying to snatch his phone out of his hand.

"Damn, Felicia, you yelling and fucking pulling on me, telling me to answer my phone.

Then, bitch, let me! Get the hell off me then." He smiled because this was his chance to clear things up.

"Hello?" He answered his phone calmly.

"Hell no, nigga, put that shit on the speaker so I can hear."

He sucked his teeth and then put the conversation on speaker.

"Hello. Is this Mr. Gary?"

Jennifer Rodriguez right away caught on to what was happening in Walt Diznee's home, so she played along to help him out.

Instead of calling him by his street name, she went professional by calling him by his government name.

Damn, this bitch is nice. And on point.

Walt Diznee looked at Felicia, who stood with her arms crossed and a smile on her face because she felt stupid.

"This is Jennifer Rodriguez at the Lopez Benz dealership," she said, and he glanced down at his watch to see the time. It was 12:21.

"Mr. Lopez needs to speak with you. He needs you to come down to the office as soon as possible."

"What's good? Was I short on the money?"

She laughed. "No, not at all, Mr. Gary. It's other reasons, sir. Trust me. It'll be worth the time. But if you can't make it tonight, I'll tell him to put it off for another time."

"Nah, nah, I'm cool with it. I'll be there in fifteen minutes. I'm heading out the door right now."

Walt Diznee hung the phone up and stuck his tongue out at Felicia in a playful way.

"Damn, boy, you make me sick." She lay on the bed and started finger-fucking herself in front of him.

"Daddy please hurry back. I'm in need of some sex therapy."

14

W HEN JENNIFER RODRIGUEZ MET Walt Diznee at the door, he noticed she was wearing a beige faux-fur vest that revealed her dark brown Stella McCartney bra. She also had on Deréon skinny jeans, bamboo hoop earrings, and light-tinted Valentino shades.

She was killing the outfit with A strappy brown Baby Phat heels to match her bra.

They greeted each other with a kiss.

"Damn, baby girl, I can't believe you came through for me earlier with that psycho bitch." Walt Diznee smiled.

"Tighten your game up, playboy. The next time, you may not be so lucky."

When she turned to walk away, Walt Diznee pulled her back for another kiss.

"Baby, you sexy as hell tonight," he told her with lustful eyes.

"You don't look too bad yourself, Mr. Gary." She grabbed his hands and led him into Mr. Lopez's office.

He glanced down and noticed a baby .380 in the waist of her pants.

Yo, what the fuck is going on? he asked himself, but he remained cool, not giving away his paranoia.

He became more nervous when they reached Mr. Lopez's office.

He was dressed in a tailored suit with Stacy Adams loafers.

"Mr. Lopez?" Jennifer called through the office door. "Mr. Gary is here, sir."

Mr. Lopez motioned for Walt Diznee to have a seat.

He offered him a cigar, but Walt Diznee refused the offer. He wanted to know what the fuck was going on and why Mr. Lopez had called him so late at night.

"Mr. Gary, I really want to get straight to the point."

He stared Walt Diznee down and then glanced over at Jennifer, who was now standing by the door.

"How do you like the Maybach?" Mr. Lopez asked. His eyes were bloodshot, as if he hadn't slept in days.

"I like it, sir."

Walt Diznee kept looking back and forth between Jennifer and Mr. Lopez. He felt uncomfortable without his pistol.

"Relax, Mr. Gary. You're safe here. Everything is fine, okay? I'll assure you of that."

Mr. Lopez didn't even crack a smile.

"Look, Mr. Lopez, I can't relax. You have me out here at a funny hour. I want to know what the fuck is going on." Walt Diznee became angry and wanted to walk out of Mr. Lopez's place of business.

"First, let me tell you a little about me. And then I'll elaborate on why I have you here in my office tonight."

Before Mr. Lopez began, he motioned for Jennifer to give them their privacy.

After she left, he continued.

"Well, as you can see, Mr. Gary, I'm not black. I'm not white," he said jokingly.

He started the conversation off to show his great personality, which was his way of breaking the ice. "Do you know anything about Nicaragua?"

Walt Diznee shook his head as if he didn't understand what Mr. Lopez was insinuating with a silly question about Nicaragua.

"Well, Nicaragua is a very small, poor country. It's the center of Central America, bordering both the Caribbean Sea and the North Pacific Ocean, between Costa Rica and Honduras.

The population is very small, only a bit over four million people. That's a wild guess.

But anyway, my mother is Nicaraguan, and my father is from Cuba. He met my mother when he came to fight in a war some years ago.

I only saw the bastard once. I was only four years old at the time when I saw him."

Mr. Lopez got up and walked to the window overlooking the city of Myrtle Beach.

He loved the city so much that after he'd visited a few years ago as a tourist with friends and family for spring break, he'd come back to buy a house, and then, later, he'd begun his Benz dealership company where notice lots of money would be made.

With his back facing Walt Diznee, he continued.

"My father walked out on my mother, leaving her to struggle. She could not work at the time.

My mother had this wooden-box vendor stand with four bicycle tires, she made it herself.

She would push her store around the neighborhood and sell coffee beans, sugar, rice, and homemade wine.

In Nicaragua, it's against the law to sell things without the government's permission."

Mr. Lopez turned back around to stare at Walt Diznee.

He sat down behind his desk, took a pull from his Cuban cigar, and then exhaled the thick clouds of blue smoke that were not good for his health, and he continued.

"There, the government is very strict and tight about a lot of things.

They caught my mother, more than once, selling products without permission.

Them bastards even threatened my ole lady, telling her she'd be tossed in jail for a long time if she didn't discontinue her illegal business."

Mr. Lopez laughed at the memories. "My mother didn't want to give birth to me in a clinic. That's why she kept selling shit. My mother never gave a fuck about the government. She wanted to have me in the hospital 'cause most kids born in the clinic came from poor families, but the ones being born in the hospital were grateful and blessed."

Walt Diznee thought about the struggle he and his family had had to endure for many years before he was old enough to run the streets.

They'd been poor, without a dime in their pockets to save their life.

He remembered how painful it had been for him and his three brothers at times, he remembered how an ice cream truck would visited their hood, and very kid in the hood was fortunate enough to have some small change in his or her pocket to purchase ice cream of his or her choice, except for Walt Diznee and his brothers.

They were the only ones without snacks to enjoy. It hurted so to watch all the other kids eat their ice cream, while they didn't have any.

"Come on, y'all. Let's go home," he'd say.

"Mom has a bowl of sugar. We can eat syrup sandwiches and drink sugar water."

The tears he fought to hold back at the painful memories, burned his eyes.

He realized after hearing Mr. Lopez's story that you might think, you had it hard in life, until you met other people.

You never knew who had it harder.

"So where was you born, Mr. Lopez?" Walt Diznee asked.

"My grandmother won the lottery, so I was one of the grateful kids." Mr. Lopez smiled.

"After my mother had me, my grandmother put her land up for collateral to get a visa.

Using the visa, she brought my mother and me, along with the rest of the lottery money to America.

My grandmother already had an older sister living in Key West, Florida, so we moved to Miami. And that's where we found our happiness."

Mr. Lopez leaned back in his chair and took a look at Walt Diznee for a quick second before continuing. "Corey, I think Jennifer likes you. She begged me to give you a chance."

"Hold on, Mr. Lopez. I must ask, What chance are you talking about? I'm lost."

He wanted to know what Jennifer was up to. He didn't want to talk about getting a job. He didn't need to work to earn his money; he had his own way of making a dollar.

He waited for Mr. Lopez to speak. *This mothafucka better not offer me no damn job, yo.*

"Do you know anything about cocaine?"

Walt Diznee paused, caught off guard by the question.

"I know a lot about cocaine."

Mr. Lopez were twisting his five-carat-stone platinum ring.

"What can you do with one hundred kilos?" Mr. Lopez's questions were live and direct. He had no time to waste.

"Well, it depends on the cost."

"I'll let you have it for eight thousand per key. Show me what you can do with that, and I'll give you more. How does that sound?"

Walt Diznee got up to reach across Mr. Lopez's desk to shake his hand.

"Mr. Lopez, it sounds too damn good." Walt Diznee kept a straight face and never cracked a smile.

Son, let me tell you something. Anytime you conduct business with anyone, don't you ever smile. You look them right in their faces without smiling. You want other businessmen to know you have big balls.

He heard his grandfather's voice while he shook Mr. Lopez's hand with a firm, tight grip.

"I know there's a lot of money here in Myrtle Beach to be made. I was taking my time to find the right man I can trust."

Mr. Lopez looked Walt Diznee in the eyes.

"Son, whatever you do, don't play me. I'll have everything ready for you in the morning. Jennifer will be calling you to let you know where to go. Until then, I want you to be very careful out there,"

They both stood, and they shook hands once more before Walt Diznee left the office.

Now that he'd found a major connection, he was going to fuck Felicia real good, go to sleep, and be ready for the next day.

He called Redeyes and Grouch the second he hopped into his Maybach.

"Yo, I need y'all to call everybody. Tell them to meet me at 4563 tomorrow. We have some major shit to talk about.

There's a lot of money out there for us to make, baby." He hung up and drove away.

$$\c$$

"Damn, that much?" Punch was nervous.

"Nigga, you complaining?" Walt Diznee asked.

"Walt Diznee, I can handle whatever you toss my way, dawg." Redeyes spoke while looking into his brother's eyes. He was surprised Walt Diznee had that much shit and wondered what might come next.

"We're going to need more time than the usual. This is a lot of shit we got, man." Redeyes spoke while smoking a blunt.

"It's all good. You feel me? We'll work on the time once we have everyone's input on pushing this work."

Walt Diznee smiled. "Grouch, what's good with you? You think you can move some of this?"

Grouch stared at the stacked-up kilos of cocaine before turning back to Walt Diznee. "This is a major shit load of dope," Grouch teased.

"Dawg, can you handle it?" Walt Diznee repeated his question.

"Isn't our daddy named Dennis? You damn right, nigga. I got this."

Punch was already thinking. He had links in New Jersey and New York with niggas he'd grown up with, and played with, when him and his brother, Freaky Ty used to live up north before they moved back down south in the midnineties.

He couldn't believe his cousin Walt Diznee had made it so far in the game—and so fast.

Only a few months ago, Walt Diznee had started with forty dollars, and he now had seven kilos of pure heroin and one hundred bricks of cocaine. The money was definitely out there to be made.

Walt Diznee had come home from prison after five years and proven it in many ways.

"This shit is pure as hell, its lot better than before." Walt Diznee nodded.

His boy Black glanced at him cause he wants to go ahead and give his boy half of the money towards the dope.

"I got a little over a hundred bands outside in the Charger right now. I'll just hit you with the rest once things begin to really move."

Walt Diznee agreed, and they all kept hitting and passing the blunt of Kush around the room while talking about the next move. They all enjoyed the business at hand.

"I got a large amount of shit. Where I got it and how I got it, is my business.

Just know I got a serious connect. It's going to be a lot of blood shed behind this shit.

Our price will be very cheap, at eighteen thousand a brick.

A lot of mothafuckas are going to go broke now that we're soon to be on top of things.

Even the feins are getting blessed. For fifty dollars, they're getting balls." Walt Diznee paused.

"Well, this dude out here named Pee Wee doing big things." He began to clap. "At least he once was."

Everyone laughed because Walt Diznee had gotten that from a movie called *Shottaz*.

"Everything that was once his, will soon be ours. We're putting down much extortion—major, major extortion.

This nigga Pee Wee isn't allowed to make money around here unless it's our shit being sold.

As a matter of fact, I'm hearing he's a pimp. We'll let him deal with his prostitution business, but when it comes to this dope shit, there's only one or two things he can do with it: smoke it or trick it. 'Cause he isn't selling it. Not around here!"

That was the moment that would earn Walt Diznee and his crew a reputation. The shipment would handle the city of Myrtle Beach, North Myrtle Beach, Georgetown, and Conway for a week.

He wanted to send a truckload to Columbia to help them after a major drug bust that had taken place on Two Notch Road two weeks ago. After making small steps in the game for many days and many nights, but today this were a giant one.

"CRISTAL WHEN ARE YOU GOING TO let me feel that pussy? I been chasing you around for months, yo."

Cristal pushed Pee Wee's hands from between her thighs. She couldn't believe how he'd just grabbed on her.

"Pee Wee, you know what? I think it's time for you to go. 'Cause you ain't gonna just put your hands on me like that." She got up and walked away from him.

"Bitch, after all that bread I've spent on you, I can't touch the pussy?"

Pee Wee was high off Gs-up, hos-down ecstasy pills when he visited Cristal.

She opened the door for him to leave, but he refused to go.

"Bitch, I'm not going anywhere," He were very angry at her, and felt as if she was playing him. He spent a lot of time with her, and still she never give in to his games.

And for the first time ever, she wanted her baby daddy.

"Mothafucka, I'm not giving you no ass. Besides, whoever told you I wanted to give you some ass anyway?

Just because you spent money on me? That's your fault. That's what you chose to do."

Pee Wee just sat there with a dumb look on his face. He wanted to slap the shit out of her.

"Nigga, you all high on ecstasy, and now you wanna fuck! Go to them bitches you got selling pussy for you.

You shouldn't have any fucking problem bustin' a nut with them always around your nasty ass."

She held the door open for him to leave, but he took his time at getting up from her couch.

"Bitch let me tell you something. One thing about me, I don't fuck with my helpers," he said angrily.

"I keep my business and pleasure away from each other."

She looked at him as if she'd rather die than fuck with Pee Wee.

What type of woman would she be if she had sex with a pimp? She always respected herself as a woman, and plans to keep the respect. People in the streets talked and the last thing she wanted was rumors getting back to Walt Diznee.

There was one thing she knew she couldn't do, and that's putting herself out there for others to talk about.

"Well, I guess you said a mouthful, Pee Wee. I'm not your business, and I'm damn sure not your pleasure.

I called your dumb ass over here to watch some movies, but you came over to fucking disrespect me."

She was upset at him and wanted him out of her apartment. She stopped yelling at him when she heard Pee Wee's phone ring.

He picked up on the second ring. After speaking to one of his homeboys, he hung up.

"Cristal, I know what's up with you. You're the type of bitch that wants a nigga to kiss your ass. Well, I'm not the one for that shit."

She laughed at him. "Pee Wee, to be honest, I didn't offer you my ass to kiss. I've asked you to leave!"

He got up to leave, but when he stepped through the door, he fell to the ground and got pistol-whipped by three men dressed in black.

They pulled Pee Wee back into Cristal's apartment, and one held her at gunpoint. She didn't understand what was going on. She peed in her pants because she feared for her life.

"Oh shit, what the fuck is going on, yo?" Pee Wee yelled.

"Shut the fuck up, playboy! You know what time it is. Run that bread."

One of the stickup boys went into his pocket, took $5,000 from Pee Wee, and then pistol-whipped him some more.

"Nigga, where the rest of that bread at?"

Cristal screamed when she saw blood. She covered her mouth to muffle the sound. Her son, Tahshawn, was in the next room, asleep.

She didn't want him to wake up and witness what was happening in their living room.

"Look, dawg, y'all got everything."

Pee Wee tried his best to get a good look at their faces, but it was hard for him to see because they kept beating him in his face.

They pulled Pee Wee's shirt off, to hog-tie his hands and feet together. They dragged him outside and hid him in the trunk of his very own car.

Before they left, they gave Cristal Pee Wee's money.

"Baby girl, listen. Don't call the police. Call the tow truck, and have his car towed. This don't have anything to do with you, okay?"

She nodded to let him know she understood. When he got outside, the stranger pulled his mask off, but Cristal's eyes were full of tears, which made it hard for her to see in the dark parking lot.

The minute they were gone, she did what she'd been told. She called the nearest towing company and then ran to the back room, where her son was sleeping.

She got in bed with him, crying, and prayed no one would ever put her through that again.

Moments later, she saw yellow flashing lights. She got up to peek out the window and noticed Pee Wee's car was being towed with him locked in the trunk. She laughed at the sight of it.

She felt as if, it was funny.

"Yeah, mothafucka, that's what you get when you disrespect us ladies." After grabbing hold of her son, she then lay down to sleep.

"Yo, Cheese, I'm telling you, dawg, that bitch had me robbed last night. I mean, think about that shit. All of a sudden, when she wanted me to leave, she opened the door, and then three mothafuckas came rushing into her spot.

None of them niggas touched this bitch, but they came at me."

Pee Wee paced back and forth, holding a bag of ice to his swollen face. He was very upset at the incident that occurred last night.

"Pee Wee, you didn't get the chance to see who they were?" Cheese asked his boss.

"Hell no, them mothafuckas had masks on. I tried to figure their voices out but couldn't."

He was aggravated, and his face felt tight.

"And you are the only one that got touched?"

Pee Wee stopped pacing and glanced at Cheese.

"Dawg, they didn't touch the bitch. And let the truth be told, I can't really remember.

But I think they gave her my fucking money."

They were distracted when they heard two names they knew being talked about on television.

Pee Wee's knees got weak, and he fell onto the couch behind him. He couldn't believe what he was hearing. His eyes were glued to the newscaster, and behind him, they saw the projects he ran his drugs through.

The Dogwood Apartments were surrounded by dogs and police officials. He couldn't believe all this was happening.

"What the fuck?" Pee Wee was shocked.

"There's no way in hell. All this shit is happening, dawg?"

Cheese turned the volume up to hear the news being displayed before them.

"Two females were killed last night. There was manual strangulation, with a deep, narrow set of ligature marks around each victim's neck, which caused brain death from oxygen deprivation before the crushed larynx terminated airflow to the lungs.

There were bruises from knuckles on the temple, and the other victim suffered a violent and extensive traumatic insult prior to her death as well."

Pee Wee and Cheese turned and stared at each other and then back at the television.

"The victims had extensive cuts and bruises, along with broken jaws; five broken ribs; and broken legs, arms, and collarbones after being dragged almost two miles by a car."

Pee Wee let his phone ring four times before he picked up.

"Yo!" he yelled into the phone.

"Pee Wee, what the fuck is going on, man? I'm looking at the news. Someone killed Ashley and Naomi last night.

Then I got a call from Flex this morning about one of the trap spots getting kicked in. They got away with seven bricks of coke and two hundred fifty thousand dollars," Spice told Pee Wee.

"Hold on. Hold the fuck on, yo. What do you mean they hit one of my trap spots and got away with seven bricks and two hundred fifty bands of my money?"

Spice kept silent over the phone. He knew Pee Wee was about to flip out.

Pee Wee closed his eyes, trying to collect his thoughts. "Spice, which spot did they hit?"

He asked calmly.

"Well, Flex worked Warren Street last night. I worked Carver Street. Everything went well there," Spice said.

"Who's on Carver Street at the moment?" Pee Wee asked.

"Well, we just changed shifts. So Ice Cream is there now."

Pee Wee tapped Cheese to get his attention. "I need you and Cheese to call everyone that's in connection with me.

Tell them tonight is the nine-eleven meeting at the Hilton Hotel. Whoever isn't there will be dealt with. Someone out there is in on our business.

This shit has to be stopped—now!"

Pee Wee hung the phone up and leaned back into his couch with his eyes shut.

Who the fuck is behind all this?

His mind ran back to the robbery that had taken place at Cristal's apartment.

That bitch is going to regret what she had done to me. Yeah, bitch, you'll see!

CHAPTER 16

MOB RECEIVED A CALL FROM WALT Diznee, who said he had a job that needed to be done.

Mob was the type of nigga he could trust to handle certain things; he'd stop whatever he had to do to be sure Walt Diznee got taken care of. Plus, Walt Diznee had paid well ever since he'd run into his major connection.

Mob glanced at the MAC-11 sitting in his lap and smiled.

Can't go to war without money.

He knew Walt Diznee had plenty of money now, and having a lot of niggas with go-hard bitches on his payroll, had helped put Walt Diznee on the top.

Mob also fucked with niggas he knew were coldblooded murderers. Some had killed so many people that if you looked them in the eyes, you could see death in their eyes.

They were killas who'd never sold dope a day in their lives.

Mob and his crew were like the IRS. If there was a drug dealer out there doing big things and playing with ten bands or better, them mothafuckas were hit.

For the right price, Mob would have taken an infant's life.

Walt Diznee wanted him to be part of his operation because every big-time dealer needed killas on his team.

Walt Diznee made them a contract, whenever Mob made his licks, he'd give away the drugs but keep the money.

He always had felt that keeping drugs was an easier way to get noticed.

A while back, Mob had gotten shot in the shoulder when he ran into a house and tried to rob someone who sold pounds of Kush, Sour Diesel, Haze, and Bubble Gum.

He hadn't known someone else was there.

When he'd turned to leave with the goods, he'd found himself in front of a shot gun.

His victim had pulled the trigger, and the blast had spun him around when he got hit in the shoulder.

Mob had played dead, hoping the mothafucka who'd shot him wouldn't reload and shoot him again.

The shooter had run out of the room, taking the pounds of loud with him.

Mob hadn't thought twice about jumping out the window. Afterward, he'd hopped into his car and rushed himself to the hospital.

He'd undergone a two-hour surgery and, two days later, checked himself out of the hospital.

Ever since Mob had gotten shot, he'd never made a move without a bulletproof vest.

When he'd first started killing, it had been about the pleasure. Now he was in it for the business.

His heart had turned cold in his years of coming up as the shortest one in his crew—the oldest but the shortest.

He loved Mob Deep and felt they had a lot in common.

Mob Deep gave short niggas hope when it came to the streets. He showed mothafuckas that little niggas got it in, laying bigger niggas down and taking what they had.

He'd started to carry the name Mob and felt it was time to begin his reputation.

At the age of ten, a homeboy had given him his first pistol. Mob's first robbery had been stealing from crackheads coming on the block to buy dope.

His first shootout had been with niggas who bitched about it.

A few years later, no one was crazy enough to mention his name the wrong way.

He had done a few bids, but he hadn't been gone long enough for anyone else to build a rep. Two years was all he had to do.

Mob hopped into his Aston Martin and pulled off, not paying any attention to his surroundings.

Two black Crown Vics pulled up beside him. Seconds later, the dark tinted windows on the Crown Vics rolled down.

He saw AR15s being forced out of the windows.

Right away, he pulled off, running the stop sign before him.

Shots shattered his back window. Bullet holes ripped through the bumper and side fenders.

His car fishtailed onto the next street as he raced to get away.

Mob glanced in the rearview mirror and noticed he was losing them. A Crown Vic didn't stand a chance against an Aston Martin sports car, which was built for speed and tough on curves.

He knew right away, that it had been a paid hit.

Someone had placed a price on his head for sure.

He pulled over and hopped out of the car and ran into the woods.

Moments later, he spotted the Crown Vic pull up and stop.

The paid hitman noticed that no one was in his car, but it was still running. "He's gone!" someone yelled.

This was Mob's chance to see the faces of the niggas who were out to kill him.

Right away, he knew the faces, and he couldn't believe ole boy was out to get him.

Mob had thought the beef between them was over with.

"That bitch-ass nigga!" He said surprisingly.

His cousin Bee Gambino had always told him, "You can't trust snakes. They bite you once, and they'll bite you twice if you let them."

Mob had put in a lot of work for his cousin Bee Gambino before the feds knocked him off.

Even though Bee Gambino was younger than he was, he had much more money.

He watched both Crown Vics pull off. He later ran out of the woods with his MAC-11 in hand when he was sure they were gone.

Before jumping back into his Aston Martin, Mob saw a note in the driver's seat. He read the note and then tossed it out the window.

"Walt Diznee, I'm tired of playing cat and mouse with this nigga Showcase. I thought the beef between us was dead some time ago."

Mob kept rubbing his head. He could never stay still when he was paranoid. His nerves were at an all-time high.

"Mob, what the fuck happened?"

He stared at Walt Diznee.

"Look, a while back, I robbed his brother, and the very same night, his brother got shot.

It put him in a wheelchair for the rest of his life. I told that nigga I didn't have shit to do with his brother being shot, but I did rob him.

It was an order, and the money was paid up front. I needed the bread.

Once the money been touched, it ain't no reneging."

Mob explained the situation to Walt Diznee as clearly as he could.

"So what did Showcase said to that?"

Before Walt Diznee got involved, he wanted to hear the history of their beef.

"The mothafucka had no other choice but to respect that, and he also said he wasn't worried about his brother being robbed. He just wanted to know about the shooting.

We drew guns on each other, and we talked it out. It was all peaceful then and there.

But now this pussy trying to fuck me over. And I don't trust the nigga right now."

He stared at Walt Diznee, trying to figure out what he was thinking.

Mob knew Showcase was somebody Walt Diznee fucked with.

That's why Mob came to him first, to let him know what was going on.

He needed to get rid of him.

"Walt Diznee, listen. I got to kill Showcase. To be real, that nigga is fucking stupid, yo.

I know his every move and hideout."

He explained the situation, hoping Walt Diznee understood him.

"Mob, to be honest, that problem is between you and him.

That was long before my time. I can't get involved.

Deal with it the best way you think it should be handled."

Walt Diznee thought it would be best if he stayed out of it altogether.

"That's not all Walt Diznee. That nigga left a note behind saying.

'A beef isn't dead until it's killed.'

Now, you tell me. What the fuck that mean?"

He looked up at Mob.

"Like I said, deal with it the best way you think it should be handled."

"Cool. But earlier, you called and said you needed to see me.

Well, I'm here, and my ears are open." He waited for Walt Diznee to respond.

"Mob, deal with Showcase, and then we'll talk."

Walt Diznee took a pull from his blunt of Kush and rested his feet on the top of his office desk.

Without saying another word, Mob left Walt Diznee, in search for Showcase.

He rode around Myrtle Beach with James and Fox, until they spotted one of Showcase's boys walking down Yupon Street.

He was heading up Fourteenth Avenue South.

"Yo, that pussy ass nigga is in that fucking apartment.

Listen, let's park at the Sea Mist Resort, 'cause we'll have to walk the rest of the way.

James, I want you to stay in the car and keep your eyes open. And the minute you see me and Fox walk out that door, pull up so we can hop in the car. You got that?"

James nodded. "I got you, Mob. Go ahead and get that shit over with."

"Come on Fox. Let's go."

They approached the apartment, hoping no one would come out before they walked in.

Mob peeked through the windows and saw no one in the front room. The television was on and loud as hell. The timing was perfect.

He motioned for Fox to go before him while he kept his eyes in the room, to be sure no one entered.

Mob already had it in his mind to peel back the wig of anyone he saw.

He followed behind Fox as he waved his pistols. They wanted to be safe about their shit.

The loud television helped them move quickly across the room and into the hall, where they saw a figure on the bed, counting money.

Mob waved his hand for Fox to stay put and keep an eye on Showcase's boy.

While he continued to walk slowly down the hall, until he saw Showcase on top of a bitch, and fucking her.

He glanced back at Fox and held up two fingers, indicating he had two bodies on his hands.

He waved for Fox to enter the room, letting him know to move in for the kill.

The minute he heard the gunfire, Mob rushed into the next room and let off two more shots. One in the back of Showcase's head, the other in Showcase's back.

The female screamed at the top of her lungs.

"Shut the fuck up, bitch." Mob pistol-whipped her until he knocked her out.

Before leaving the room, he sent more shots at Showcase to be sure he was dead. He didn't want him coming back for any revenge.

"You ain't going to have me looking over my shoulder.

Yo Fox, let's get the fuck out of here, man."

Mob ran past Fox and noticed a large bag of money and dope.

"Fox, take the money, but leave all the dope. Hurry, man.

Let's get the fuck out, as a matter of fact, bring the dope. All that shit goes to Walt Diznee." They ran outside and saw James.

Mob and Fox hopped into the car, and James sped off onto the busy highway, and headed toward North Myrtle Beach.

Stupid nigga brought that shit on himself.

"Yo Fox, roll the fuck up, man!" yelled Mob.

I T WAS IN THE MIDAFTERNOON WHEN Grouch and Walt Diznee went out to eat at the Pan American diner.

They both ordered a shrimp-and-egg omelet with yellow rice.

They took a window booth facing Kings Highway, enjoying the busy traffic.

Wednesday was always one of their busiest days.

Walt Diznee had just opened his eighteenth trap spot on Bella Street, and it ran smoothly.

It had been a little more than four months since he and Mr. Lopez had dealt with each other.

Mr. Lopez had fallen in love with him after their first business and wished to continue his business with Walt Diznee.

Once a month, Walt Diznee would report to Mr. Lopez with more than $800,000 in drug money to work off his consignment pay.

Grouch then glanced up when he saw Redeyes walking through the doors as if being late didn't matter.

Redeyes sat down and ordered a glass of orange juice. He wasn't in the mood to eat.

They gave each other daps and began talking.

"So what do y'all think about the team?" Walt Diznee asked, looking around.

"To be honest, dawg, ya boy Cheese been acting funny lately. He barely come around, and when he do, it seems as if he's on some other shit."

Grouch took a sip from his orange juice.

"Walt Diznee, Grouch isn't lying. I be seeing that shit about him," Redeyes spoke with confirmation.

And wanted to be sure to backed up what his brother Grouch have told Walt Disney.

Walt Diznee stared out at the busy highway before speaking.

"Maybe Cheese is a bit under pressure at the moment. I mean, business has been moving nonstop these past few months, and it's looking to pick up really soon.

Cheese been doing good; he's never short on the money, and he's always on time."

Redeyes and Grouch stared at each other as if their big brother didn't understand.

"I got the both of y'all here for a reason. Me and Mr. Lopez was doing some talking the other day about this next shipment."

Walt Diznee looked around the diner before he continued.

"Man, this shipment is huge. Mr. Lopez wants me to start pushing our shit throughout North Carolina." He slightly smiled.

"Walt Diznee, are you fucking crazy?" Grouch whispered.

"Nigga, you already know that's Teflon's area."

"I know, Grouch. Just listen to me, please.

Damn, that's why I've called y'all here. So we can figure something out."

Walt Diznee was calm and collected, trying his best to speak with a clear mind.

"Walt Diznee, what is there to figure out?" Redeyes asked.

"Look, man, I think I need to have a talk with Teflon. Maybe he'll go against his rule about not putting his family and business together.

I mean, look at us. We're doing big things out here right now, and that's without his help." Walt Diznee smiled.

"Yeah, and you got to understand that ever since you came in power, a lot of mothafuckas started popping up either missing or dead. And you really think that Teflon don't know about that shit?"

Grouch leaned back, waiting for Walt Diznee to respond.

"What the fuck all that got to do with me and Teflon becoming partners?"

"I'll tell you what the fuck it has to do with it." Redeyes jumped in.

"Teflon is going to look at the facts of him letting you in, could be a problem.

Because he's been running North Carolina at a good pace for a long time.

If Teflon lets you in, it's going to be World War Three if he fucks with you Walt." Redeyes took a sip from his drink.

"Nigga you are going to be power struck, and a lot of things can happen behind that."

Walt Diznee wanted to be the next Frank Matthews, he had made the city of Myrtle Beach a murder capital.

There was an average of four to five drug-related deaths per day.

There were so many bodies that the medical examiner had to buy a refrigerated van to regularly house the overflow of death.

Walt Diznee had bought more luxury cars, including a Rolls-Royce Phantom Coupé and a Porsche Panamera, and had redone the interior of his Maybach in Gucci.

He was another black gangster living the high-style life he'd dreamed of so many years while in prison.

Grouch glanced at Redeyes before he spoke. "Walt Diznee, listen, man. Whenever you came home and got back in the game, it was all about stacking that bread and getting your family back.

Me and Redeyes were with you on that.

But now it's getting out of hands man.

You have over two hundred employees working for you. Seventy percent of them are soldiers.

The other thirty percent is pushing drugs."

Grouch spoke in a soft tone. He didn't want anyone around them to hear their conversation.

"Hold up, my dawg. I came to talk about the next shipment Mr. Lopez is soon to have in a few weeks, and y'all mothafuckas talking about the killing that's going on around us.

I don't want to hear that bullshit. That shit comes with the street life we're living.

Some of us get money, some of us get pussy, some of us get put in jail, and some of us get killed." Walt Diznee paused.

"Man, look, do y'all want to know what's going on or not?" he asked.

Grouch and Redeyes sat quietly.

"Damn… Can y'all please let me finish, 'cause I really need y'all's input on this, and that's why I came to y'all.

There's over two thousand kilos of cocaine out there that's being divided between Mr. Lopez and his two brothers.

Half comes here; half goes to Dallas, Texas; and the rest goes to Miami.

Mr. Lopez said this is the biggest shipment so far."

Walt Diznee leaned back in his booth seat and took a bite of his omelet.

"Walt Diznee, why couldn't you just tell him that North Carolina is being supplied by someone else? And this shipment is too large for you to handle.

He shouldn't order so much shit at one time."

Grouch tried his best to convince his brother to end the deal with his supplier.

"Look, that's what I told him. But he was saying some shit about Obama and the president over in Mexico is making a speech in a few months about putting tighter security on the border to stop guns and dope coming into the States.

So he had no other choice."

Walt Diznee kept looking from one brother to the other.

"So you're going to talk to Teflon about needing his help?" Redeyes asked.

"There's only one or two things Teflon can say, and that's yes or no.

Look, I don't need North Carolina is what I'm trying to tell y'all.

I mean, I do but only for the shipment that's coming in really soon. After that, things should be running smooth again."

They sat and talked for hours about the dos and don'ts with the next shipment.

As a group, they had a lot of agreements and disagreements, but no one left until everyone was at peace with the upcoming business.

"You converse with Tef. If he agrees, then I'm in," Grouch said.

"And count me in too," Redeyes said.

"But Tef has to agree to it, Walt." Grouch insured him.

Teflon was at home in his new four-thousand-square-foot duplex house, when he welcomed his brother Walt Diznee through the security gate.

He had a circular driveway surrounded by numerous palm trees and manicured grass that covered ten acres of land.

Walt Diznee then pulled up behind Teflon's all-white Bugatti.

Damn, my big brother is living.

He got out to meet his brother at the top of his circular steps.

Teflon looked small compared to the two large columns and French doors behind him. "What up, Teflon?"

"What up, li'l' bro?"

They entered the large duplex home, and a butler greeted them.

"Would you like to have anything to drink, sir?" The butler asked.

"Sure, we'll have glasses of Ace of Spades, please."

Teflon walked towards a door that led them into a hallway that had dim cup lights in the ceiling above them.

Walt Diznee couldn't believe his eyes when he stepped into a home theater for the first time.

American Gangster was playing on the large projector screen.

The theater was spacious and contained seven recliners, a popcorn machine, and a Jacuzzi for two.

It even had two separate restrooms: one for gentlemen and the other for ladies.

"Damn, it's just like the real movies."

What amazed Walt Diznee the most, was the plush all-white carpet beneath his feet.

He had to remove his Mauri gator loafers before entering the home theater.

They sat down, and the butler served their drinks.

"So, little brother, what brought you over here?" Teflon was being sarcastic.

"Damn, Teflon, why can't I just come over and visit? Does it really have to be any reason?"

Teflon glanced over at his brother, to show he knew, he'd came over for something and not just a visit.

"Teflon, I'm really feeling this my dawg. You living big-time, nigga.

How many square feet is it?"

Teflon saw the excitement in his brother's eyes. It was Walt Diznee's first time seeing the new home.

"It's only four thousand. That's it," Teflon said.

"Grouch and Redeyes told me you have a nice home too." Teflon smiled.

"Yeah, it's aight. You got me beat by two thousand square feet, though." They both laughed.

"Fuck you, Teflon." Walt Diznee stuck his middle finger up.

"What! What I did Walt Diznee? Why it got to be 'Fuck me,' stupid nigga?

Hell, I can't help it if my money longer than yours."

His brother Teflon teased.

"Yeah, mothafucka, I got to give you props. You doing your thing.

But you best believe your little brother's playing with millions too, mothafucka. So don't get it fucked up, nigga."

He spoke highly of himself.

"Yeah, but the man's right here." Teflon smiled and thumbed himself in the chest.

It felt good to laugh and joke with each other.

For many years, Walt Diznee had prayed for those days to come back, when they could play, laugh, and have fun like when they were kids.

The streets had robbed them both of their childhood years, forcing them to become men and being a bit more serious when it came to money.

It was the first time they had sat and laughed with each other, and it felt good.

"Teflon, when was the last time you heard from Mama and Daddy?" Walt Diznee asked.

"I been by there today. Why?"

"How they doing?" Walt Diznee wondered.

He haven't seen his mother and father in a week now.

Teflon smiled. "They're cool. Mama enjoys our street wealth to the fullest."

"Shit, I don't blame her. She know she don't have to work for the rest of her years now."

Walt Diznee felt proud knowing they could do anything they wanted for their mother and father.

But back then, shit was rough.

"I know Corey, but Daddy still doing him, working like there's no tomorrow."

"Man, you got to understand our old man got a hard head.

Do you know who his damn daddy was?"

Walt Diznee smiled, and they laughed at the memories of their granddaddy and how he'd hustled his ass off to get money.

"And, Teflon, you know you couldn't tell Granddaddy shit. He was going to do him regardless."

The both of them had really missed their grandfather.

"Yeah, you're right. If he's pleased with working, then I guess we'll have to let him work, li'l' bro."

Walt Diznee sat looking at the projector screen before bringing up the issue he really needed to talk about.

He wanted to be sure he was doing the right thing and not invading his brother's space.

And there's only one way of finding out if his brother Teflon would be okay with his plans.

"Teflon, to be honest, I did come over to speak with you about a very important issue I'm soon to be dealing with.

But before you say anything, at least hear me out."

Teflon shut his eyes and leaned his head back on the chair.

"I fucking knew it. I knew it. I knew it."

Teflon laughed.

He released a chestful of air as if he were exhausted.

Walt Diznee hated the reaction, and it startled him to see his big brother's frustrated expression.

"Okay, what is it you want to talk about now?" Teflon asked.

"I got this major connect I've been dealing with for some time now, and the shit I've been getting from him lately is real fucking good.

Half the shit that's on the streets now came from him through me.

No one knows who I'm dealing with other than Grouch and Redeyes, and I'm keeping it that way. You feel me?

But as of right now, what I really want to talk to you about is—"

He paused for a moment before speaking.

"Fuck it. Look, man, I know you have a rule about not putting your family and business together, but—"

Teflon held his hands up to stop the conversation.

"Wait a minute. Are you coming up in here to talk to me about street business? 'Cause if so, I'm not trying to hear it, man." Teflon shook his head.

"Teflon, please just hear me out. I need your help!" Walt Diznee yelled.

They both sat quietly staring at each other.

"I'm not asking for anything out of your reach, Teflon. I talked with my people a few days ago.

He has a large truckload of dope coming in a few weeks, with about two thousand bricks.

It's being split up between him and his other two brothers in other states.

His shipment is being hauled here to Myrtle Beach.

He told me this was the biggest shipment ever. Because Obama and the president in Mexico are about to make a big speech about putting heavier security on the border to stop guns coming into the States." Walt Diznee explained the movement he had lined up.

All he needed was Teflon's consent.

"Okay, what does that got to do with me?"

Walt Diznee smiled.

He knew that when his brother asked a question, he had a greater chance of winning him over.

"Okay, Teflon, listen. I'm not asking you to become my partner. I just need you to help me move this load.

South Carolina isn't going to need all that shit. I was thinking maybe you could let me move some of it in North Carolina."

Teflon stared at the wide projector screen as if he hadn't heard one word his brother had said.

Then he turned to face Walt Diznee.

"Mothafucka, let me tell you something. I'm going to do this one for you, and this is it.

I'll let you have Wilmington, Lumberton, and Fayetteville, and that's only because I'm taking a few weeks off from the game.

So I want my ten percent cut off each city."

"Damn, Teflon, that's thirty percent."

Teflon looked up with a smile on his face.

"Walt Diznee, it's either some or none. You make the call."

He left the decision to his brother.

Walt Diznee took a sip from his drink and stood. "Fuck it. Deal!"

18

WALT DIZNEE WAS HEADING HOME, when he got a call about his cousin Punch had just been killed.

Punch had been traveling on Highway 31, heading north toward Atlantic Beach, around five thirty in the afternoon.

His assassins had pulled up beside his Audi and opened fire. It had been a drive-by at top speed.

People in the moving traffic had witnessed what took place in broad daylight.

Punch's car had spun out of control and crashed into the concrete wall.

The impact had caused him to be crushed instantaneously.

He had been large: six foot seven and 240 pounds.

It hurt Walt Diznee to hear about the death of his big cousin.

Right away, he started making calls and sending out orders to find out who'd put a hit on his cousin.

Whoever done this will fucking pay.

Tears ran down his face.

He'd been heading home to his girl when he got the call, and now he changed his mind.

He did not want to go to his grandmother's house either.

Cause he knew all his aunts, uncles, and cousins would be there.

He felt better being alone in his car, driving nowhere, it'd help to clear his mind.

His thoughts wandered to his baby mama, he missed them being together as a family and loved her so much that his thoughts of her overrode the death of his cousin Punch.

The thing that bothered him most was the memory of seeing Cristal with Pee Wee.

He wanted to destroy everything Pee Wee had.

A few nights ago, he'd had Pee Wee robbed, and then he'd run into one of his crack spots and dragged two of Pee Wee's bitches throughout the projects for everyone to see.

Walt Diznee knew that, dropping the price of his dope being sold, Pee Wee's business would slow down.

He smiled at the idea of it all.

He was now playing in the big league!

But the thought of being in prison with no canteen money and only surviving month to month with indigent packages that the state provided for him made his heart flutter.

Yeah, I bet them niggas wouldn't think I'd be out here doing it up!

He rented out three of his heroin spots to niggas in Virginia.

Fifty thousand a month was his offer to them.

He knew they'd see their money back off one trap spot in two weeks or less.

His boy Showcase came across his mind as well.

It hurted him to know he was dead now.

Showcase had always been good to him, but it was a street rule that you lived by the gun and would die by it.

Walt Diznee could have spared his life, but he felt that if Showcase had made a deal with Mob and later crossed him, he might one day, double cross Walt Diznee too.

He put himself in Mob's shoes.

Being shot at wasn't something you could just put aside, so Walt Diznee had stepped back and let Mob and Showcase deal with their longtime beef once and for all.

He decided to drive by his baby mother's apartment complex to see if her car was in the parking lot.

He went down Airport Road, turned left onto Highway 15, and then took a right by Town Square Apartments.

He was now heading toward Carolina Cove.

When he got to her apartment, he noticed two females surrounding Cristal and his son, Tahshawn.

One of them grabbed Cristal from behind, and the other hit her in the face.

He saw his son trying his best to help his mother, but the seven-year-old's efforts were worthless.

Before he could jump out of the car, the second female pulled out a box cutter and sliced Cristal across the chest.

The two females then ran away and hopped into a hot-pink 4.6 Range Rover.

They sped away, leaving Cristal on the ground, badly wounded.

Tahshawn cried and reached for his mother, he than notice blood pouring from his mother's chest.

"Tahshawn, get in the car while I grab your mother!"

His son's face lit up with excitement, although he feared for his mother's life. "Daddy!"

Tahshawn yelled. "Okay, Daddy!"

"It's okay, Cristal. I got you. Just don't die on us.

I'm taking you to the hospital, okay?"

He put Cristal in the backseat of his Maybach, not worried about the blood staining the seat.

He wanted to save her!

"Daddy, is Mama okay?"

Tahshawn kept looking in the backseat to watch over his mother.

He saw his mother's blood pouring out of her chest.

She was screaming.

Cristal couldn't believe she was about to lose her life to a box cutter.

"Corey, please don't let me die! Help me, Corey. Please don't let me die."

She begged him not to let her lose her life.

She wanted to be there to see their only son become a man.

Streams of tears ran down her face, mixing with the smudges of blood that covered her cheeks.

Walt Diznee took the back way out of the Carolina Cove apartment complex onto Kings Highway.

He took Business Twelfth Avenue South, running red lights all the way up Twenty-First Avenue North. He made a left onto highway 17 until he reached the Grandstand Hospital.

Within fifteen minutes, as they raced to the hospital, Cristal had passed out.

He ran through the emergency room's glass sliding doors, yelling for help. Moments later, four nurses ran outside and noticed Cristal lying unconscious, covered with blood.

They rushed her to the surgical room right away.

Walt Diznee hugged his son. "Tahshawn, everything's going to be okay now.

These people will take care of her. We're not going to lose her. I promise! Your mother's strong."

♀

Hours later, Walt Diznee and his son fell asleep on the lobby sofa after staying up late worrying about Cristal.

He turned his phone off because he didn't want to be bothered at the moment.

It hurt him to see her in the condition she was in. But he knew this could be his chance to show her how much he really cared for her.

He could have the talk with her he'd spent so many years begging God for.

Why had she left him?

He knew he'd made a mistake, but damn, what had he done to make her hate him so much? He wanted Cristal to open her eyes and see that she'd never find another man who could love her and care for her the way he did.

He needed her to understand that her neglecting him had made him who he was now: a successful big-time drug dealer, a millionaire of the streets. But he was weak. He'd felt that way during his five years without her.

When he'd come home from prison, he'd tried to move on without her, but it had hurt too badly.

He wanted both her, and Tahshawn back in his life.

The feeling of being neglected had given him the push and motivation to get back in the game and show her he could do without the powder sniffing and being in and out of jail.

He wanted to show her that he had gone to prison as a boy but come home as a man.

He wanted to show her how badly he wanted his family back. Being a big-time drug dealer wasn't his plan.

He felt a tap on his shoulder that woke him up.

He looked around and noticed his son had fallen asleep next to him.

"Excuse me, sir."

Walt Diznee looked up and saw a male surgeon.

"Sorry to wake you," the doctor said.

"No, you're okay, sir. I must've fell asleep without knowing." Walt Diznee cleared his throat and rubbed his eyes.

The surgeon smiled. "You saved her life. She has been sliced across the chest, and the cut grazed the lungs, missing the heart by two inches.

The loss of blood caused her to black out. If you hadn't gotten here in time, she would have died."

Walt Diznee looked over at his son, who was now awake.

"Well, when can we see her, Doc? I'm pretty sure she'll be happy to see us."

"No problem. Are you related to Ms. Homely, by any chance?"

Walt Diznee paused for a minute.

"Yes, sir, I'm her baby father. This is our son, Tahshawn." Walt Diznee smiled.

"Well, if you would like to see her, please go through those double doors to the right.

You'll take the elevator to the fourth floor, or take the stairs, whichever one you prefer.

It'll be the fifth room on the right, sir."

Walt Diznee shook the doctor's hand and went toward the double doors.

"Daddy, can we use the elevator?" His son was pulling him in the direction of the elevator so he could get a few seconds of fun riding up.

"Yeah, Tahshawn, 'cause I'm not walking up four flights of stairs. Fuck that shit."

Moments after the elevator ride, they entered her room, they saw Cristal lying in the hospital bed.

Tubes ran into her nose, and needles with morphine drips had been placed in her arms.

Walt Diznee walked closer to her bed, where his son was now standing.

Her eyes opened.

She tried to focus on the walls around her and then looked up at Walt Diznee. Then she turned to face their son, Tahshawn, who stared down at her.

"Oh, Tahshawn," she whispered. She was weak. Her lips were ashy white.

"Hi, Mama." Tahshawn felt bad for his mother.

She reached over to touch him on the chin and smiled a weak smile.

"Taters."

Her weak voice was low and hoarse.

Walt Diznee filled a cup with water and then placed a flexible straw inside for her to sip on.

"Here you go. Drink some water." He leaned over to help put the straw between her dry lips.

She was so drugged up that only after she sipped the water did she notice her son's father.

"Corey, what are you doing here?" She rolled her eyes and turned her head away from him.

"I'm the one that brought you to the hospital, remember?"

He tried to help her remember what had taken place.

"I'm talking about my room."

Walt Diznee looked down at his son and then back up into Cristal's weak eyes.

"I just wanted to see if you're okay. I haven't called your mom and them yet."

He set the cup of water on the hospital table.

"The doctor told me I got you here just in time. If I hadn't, you would've died."

She turned her head to face him. Tears ran down her face.

"The doctor said you blacked out. You lost a lot of blood." He looked down at her.

"Cristal, what the fuck happened? Why those bitches cut you?"

She lay quietly, not saying anything.

She felt embarrassed about what had taken place and that it had happened right in front of Walt Diznee.

It hurt her more than anything in the world that it also had happened in front of their son.

"I had company at my apartment the other night," she said finally.

"He started grabbing on me the wrong way, like I was one of his bitches. So I asked him to leave.

But the minute I opened the door for him to leave, three men came busting in and started to beat him up.

They took all his money.

So now he's thinking I had something to do with that shit, when I don't.

So he sent them bitches at me.

I told them it wasn't my fault that shit happened to him. They didn't believe me."

Cristal started crying.

Walt Diznee felt bad, he knew that was his fault she'd gotten sliced across her chest.

Now he had no choice but to get involved. He wanted his cousin to take Pee Wee out.

Yeah, I'm going to let Shae Shae take his ass out. He thought to himself.

"You can't go back to that apartment. Plus, the doctor said you'll be leaving in a week or so, and you have to be supervised.

You might have to stay with me until you get better."

Their son jumped up and down with excitement written all over his face.

"Please, Mama? Can we stay with Daddy? He said I have my own room with a big bed and a flat-screen TV. Please, Mama, can we stay?"

Cristal knew if she went back to her apartment, those bitches would be back.

So she agreed to move in with him, only until she found a better place to live.

But on the other hand, she wanted to find out how her son's father was living.

She wanted to be nosy.

"Okay, Corey, but I'm telling you right now. Don't get any wrong ideas about this shit." She rolled her eyes.

"Girl, shut the fuck up. I just want to help you," he lied.

Don't worry, boo boo. As soon as you get well, I'll be in that pussy again.

"Here baby, drink some more water." He smiled.

CHAPTER 19

W ALT DIZNEE CALLED HIS COUSIN Shae Shae because he knew she would be perfect for the hit.

He put up $50,000 to have Pee Wee killed.

Shae Shae lived up north, where she'd become part of the Blood nation.

Due to her dedication and loyalty, she put in major work for her nation.

She'd later formed her own crew of Bloodettes, and called themselves the Ruby Queens.

Everyone who knew them, called them PSD. Which meant for Pretty, Sexy, and Dangerous.

They all dressed classy, as if they lived on *Rip the Runway*.

They all had baby faces that made them look young and innocent.

The Ruby Queens grabbed the attention of any man who laid eyes on them, and if he was not careful, he would be their next lick.

The Ruby Queens had rules. They would not sleep with any man. Strictly pussy!

Shae Shae was the head of things. She was the mastermind behind everything.

One day they robbed a big-time drug dealer and took everything he had.

When he found out the PSD were behind the robbery, he paid young Jack Boys who were trying to build a reputation for themselves, to take out Shae Shae and her crew.

When Shae Shae and her girls were standing on the block in Harlem, on 126th, an unexpected drive-by came through.

They all got hit and were rushed to the hospital, where Shae Shae was in a coma for a month.

She woke up to the bad news that her friends hadn't made it.

She couldn't believe what she was hearing.

She thought she was dreaming while in her coma, and the devastated news she's hearing, are driving her crazy.

She'd missed her girls' funerals and hadn't gotten to see their faces for the last time.

Twice a year, she visited them for an hour at their grave sites, every since she was released from the hospital.

She never brought any roses because roses were the same as human beings, they'll blossomed to be as charming, as any life has to offer.

But eventually, they'll die from the lack of moisture and, turning black and lifeless, then soon withers away.

She wanted to buy some artificial ones, but those could be as painful as the real roses.

They'll get blown away and lost in a storm.

Shae Shae didn't want to bring anything that would remind her of the losses.

Instead, she came empty-handed with only love, that would never die or be blown away in the roughest storm.

Her heart had turned black and cold against life.

Without her girls, she thought, *Fuck the world!*

She was in her new BMW 745Li, when she passed the Welcoming sign that says, Welcome to Myrtle Beach sign.

She pulled up to the red traffic light and turned onto Twenty-First Avenue, leaving Business 17.

Walt Diznee had gotten her a spot at the Marriott long enough for her to complete her hit.

She'd brought her side kick with her.

Young Mafio was her soldier, and she always kept him close to her.

"Mafio, I got to get ready.

Walt Diznee wants me to meet him at Club Isis tonight.

They're throwing a big birthday bash for him.

Do you want to come?"

she asked while hiding her gun on her hip.

"Nah, baby girl, I'm chillin' so I can get some rest. Besides, you know I can't party with these country people," Young Mafio teased.

"Boy, shut up. My damn cousins isn't country." She laughed at Young Mafio.

"Well, isn't this the South?" he asked jokingly.

"The only thing I want to do is make this lick and head back up north, Shae Shae."

"Well, probably tomorrow cause my cousin have to let us know what to do and, we'll go from there."

She looked herself over once more in the large body mirror.

She wanted to be the flyest bitch in the club. And put on an outfit she knew hadn't come out yet in the South.

When she got to club Isis, she saw it was packed from wall to wall.

The minute she entered the club, she went in search of her cousins. They hadn't seen each other in years, but always kept in touch by phone.

She smiled when she saw Teflon, Walt Diznee, Grouch, and Redeyes posing with Buffie the Body to take a picture.

Walt Diznee and his brothers were fly as hell.

He had on a Gucci dual-time digital watch and a tonal embroidered cable-knit sweater.

He wore a fitted hat that went with his pants, all made by Crown Holder. He even had the Sean John shades to match.

Redeyes and Grouch both rocked Konvict outfits.

They looked like twins.

The only difference was the color of the outfit. They even wore the same style of Mauri loafers.

Teflon was sharp in the black-label jeans, a button-up shirt, and his Cartier watch.

Shae Shae walked up to them from the side and jumped into their picture before it snapped.

"Oh shit, what's up, dawg?" yelled Grouch.

"Shae Shae, what the fuck you doing down here, yo?"

"Damn, can I come chill with my cousins sometime, What? I don't belong down south or something?" she asked jokingly, and reached over to give them all a hug.

"I'm seeing y'all doing real good down here. Y'all niggas ballin' hard." She smiled a wide smile.

"Damn, let us get some love. Hell, you already fucked my birthday picture up," Walt Diznee joked.

Walt Diznee and Teflon grabbed Shae Shae in a group hug.

"Happy birthday, Walt Diznee. I'm seeing you got a lot of love tonight. It's packed as hell in here," she said.

He shook his head in a disbelieving way, took a sip of his cup, and then glanced across the crowd.

"These mothafuckas don't love me. Hell, half these people don't even know me.

I'm throwing a gangsta party with free champagne, and a celebrity. That's why they're here."

Walt Diznee paused for a second. "What the fuck?"

Shae Shae turned her head in the direction Walt Diznee was looking, but the crowd was too thick for her to spot what he was looking at.

"Shae Shae, come with me," Without speaking another word, he walk off.

They were heading in the direction that caught Walt Diznee's attention.

"What the fuck are you doing out here?" he spoke to her angrily.

"I'm okay. The doctor told me not to drink any alcohol. So please go have your fun."

He knew she was lying about talking to her doctor, but he didn't say anything.

"Don't you know them bitches you had it out with a few weeks ago, might be out here."

She cut her eyes as if he were aggravating her.

He saw the expression and walked away, pulling Shae Shae to the side. He whispered,

"I know I called you down here for another mission, but while you're here, I need you to keep an eye on my baby mother."

He looked his cousin in the eyes and waited for her to response.

"I tell you what. If it bothers you that much, this'll be my gift to you.

Happy birthday nicca!"

Shae Shae smiled and winked.

"Thanks."

And without saying another word, he walked off heading back toward his brothers, while she kept close to Cristal.

Shae Shae followed his baby mother to the bar but slowed down when she noticed Cristal being approached by two other girls.

She eased herself closer.

"Yeah, bitch, I see that slice across your chest wasn't deep enough."

Cristal grabbed Lania by the hair, spit a razor out of her mouth, and began slicing her in the face.

Before the other female could grab Cristal from behind, Shae Shae grabbed her by the arm, and let off two shots into her ribs.

When the crowd ran for the door, Shae Shae grabbed Cristal.

The both of them ran with the crowd, after she pulled her wig off and tossed it away.

They met up with Walt Diznee at the door.

Without stopping, Shae Shae kept walking towards her car and pulled off with ease, and unnoticed.

"What the fuck is going on in the club, yo?" Cheese asked.

Him and Pee Wee were sitting in the club's parking lot in their car, smoking loud when they heard everyone yelling.

Pee Wee leaned up to see what Cheese was talking about.

"Oh shit, look at that bitch Cristal. And who in the fuck she's with Cheese.

Who the fuck them niggas is, she's with?"

Pee wee asked the same question twice.

He couldn't believe he's seeing her again.

"That's them clown-ass niggas I was telling you about.

You see the dude that's holding Cristal's hand? Well, that's her baby daddy, Walt Diznee.

Now look behind them, Cristal and her baby daddy.

Those two niggas is his brothers, Grouch and Redeyes.

Now, the main one I was telling you about, is that nigga Teflon.

He's the one posted up in front of the all-white Bugatti.

That's the one with all the money, and I'm surprised to even see that nigga at a club.

He don't fuck around with clubs at all."

Cheese pointed out Walt Diznee and his crew of brothers.

"Yo, Cheese, what the fuck happened to Lania and Toya. I don't see any of them bitches yo."

CHAPTER 20

E ARLY THE NEXT MORNING, PEE WEE got a call from Lania. She was at Georgetown Memorial.

Cristal had sliced her face badly.

Her beauty was now gone. It bothered her a lot that Pee Wee might no longer needed her anymore.

He was a pimp and only dealt with beautiful and sexy bitches.

Even though he wouldn't be able to make money off her, she could still be one of his soldiers in the battlefield, she hoped.

The thought of being cast away brought tears to her eyes.

"Hello?" Pee Wee answered.

"Pee Wee, this me—Lania," she said.

"Lania, what the fuck happened last night at the club? I noticed everyone came running outside like that shit caught on fire.

And the next thing I know, I saw you ran out with your face covered in blood. And we didn't saw Toya.

When me and Cheese saw the ambulance, we left.

We knew the police were going to be there, and we had work on us."

Lania began to cry. "Pee Wee, Toya is dead."

The bad news fucked him up. He couldn't believe it.

"Dead? What the fuck are you talking about, Lania?" He felt confused and wanted her to be a bit more specific.

"Pee Wee, last night me and Toya spotted that bitch Cristal at the bar, so I approached the her.

We had a few words, and the next thing I knew, she grabbed my hair and then started to cut me in the fucking face with a box razor while punching me at the same time.

Then I heard a gun go off right next to me. Everybody started to run.

When I looked down, Toya was already lying on the floor.

And that's when I realized it was her that got shot!" she cried.

"So who fucking shot her?"

"Pee Wee, that's the problem. At the moment, your little bitch Cristal had my hair and was pulling my head down, so I really didn't see shit.

Plus, I had a lot of blood in my eyes."

Pee Wee stayed quiet.

"Well, when the ambulance got there, Toya was still alive, but by the time we got to the hospital in Georgetown, she was dead." Lania was hurt.

Her best friend she'd met through Pee Wee was now gone.

"Hey, Lania, remember that dude Walt Diznee that Cheese was telling us about? Well, we spotted that bitch with him and his brothers last night.

And I'm losing a lot of money with that nigga around. Fuck that shit! He got to go. And that money-hungry ho is going with him."

Pee Wee hung up with Lania and dialed Cristal's number. Her phone rang and then went to voice mail.

He was determined to find her, he wanted her dead!

Pee Wee hit a few keys on his phone to enable the chaperone feature.

He stared at the map and waited until an address appears onto his cellphone.

Yeah, bitch, you can run, but you can't fucking hide.

Cristal wanted to make things better between her and Walt Diznee.

She kept telling herself she couldn't always go on being hard on him.

He'd taken her in and taken care of her until she got better.

She knew how he felt for her, and she felt bad about the way she'd treated him.

He was the perfect father.

He spoiled their son with everything he wanted.

Seeing their son happy had opened her eyes to starting things over with him.

She felt safe around her baby daddy. He was the king on his chessboard, and she wanted to be his queen.

She couldn't believe the way he was living.

She'd never thought she would see the day. She looked around the huge estate and couldn't help but smile.

All day, she would walk around his house and admire the beauty. She'd always dreamed of living in a two-story home, and there she was, standing in a two-story five-bedroom home with four and a half baths and a bar for visitors, which he barely had. She fell in love with the romantic environment.

She wanted to cook him and their son a nice, special meal.

She grabbed his apron, that has "Walt Diznee" on the front.

And she already knew he didn't eat pork or red meat.

He kept only fish, chicken, and turkey products in the refrigerator.

She smiled at the thought of him eating her pussy. *I bet he'll eat this red meat.* She jumped at a knock on the door. She wondered who it might be.

She and Tahshawn had been there for a little more than a month, and not once had anybody come by without notice.

"Who is it?" She opened the door, and to her surprise, it was a female. *Really!* she thought.

They just stood there not saying a word. Cristal couldn't believe how cute she was.

Right away, she cussed herself for not being dressed for a time like that.

This must be one of Corey's bitches.

She felt a bit of jealousy coming on. She smiled to help hide her insecurity. She saw the envy in Felicia's face.

She couldn't do anything to hide the hurt in her eyes.

Felicia kept looking Cristal up and down. But what caught her attention the most was the child who reminded her of her lover—his head, his eyes, and his nose.

He stood beside his mother, looking up at her. Felicia wanted to cry, but the pain wouldn't let her. *That must be his son.*

"Uh, excuse me?" Cristal said. "Are you looking for someone?"

Felicia just stood there for a second before speaking. "Is Walt Diznee home?"

"No, Corey, isn't here at the moment," Cristal told her.

"Well, you must be his sister?"

Cristal knew it was a trick question, so she gave Felicia a tricky answer. "No, honey, I'm his baby mother, and you must be his insurance collector.

Look, you need to get to the point of why you are here, 'cause I have things that need to be done before my baby daddy gets home."

Cristal wanted to bust out laughing at her own joke, but she held it in.

"No, I'm not his insurance collector. My name is Felicia. I'm his lady friend.

So where is Walt Diznee, and why do you have the apron on I bought for him?"

She noticed Cristal had written on the apron, which now said, "Walt Diznee Girl."

"Well, like I said, Corey isn't here. He never told me anything about you or him having a lady friend.

And the reason I have this apron on is because I was about to cook him a vegetarian lasagna and fried onion rings for dinner. Since you must know."

Felicia wanted to spit in her face, but she didn't want to be disrespectful in front of their son. "Well, you tell Walt Diznee or Corey or whoever the hell he might be that Felicia came by.

Tell him I'm done with all his bullshit. I went out of town for a business meeting, and here it is.

He got you living with him?" Felicia was upset about seeing another woman in Walt Diznee's home—a woman who'd borne his only child, his family.

"Well, is that all, ma'am? 'Cause I really have to start cooking. I would hate to have my baby daddy return home to an empty kitchen," Cristal teased.

"Bitch, you're lucky your son's standing here." Felicia stormed away with her fist balled up. She couldn't believe his baby mother had tried to play her.

Cristal closed the door, smiling, and knew Felicia would have be upset, seeing her there.

Whenever Walt Diznee came home, she would have to hear him fuss about his li'l' bitch, but she couldn't have cared less.

She wanted to call her best friend, Pam, to tell her what had just taken place, but instead, she got dressed to go to the food market.

She wanted to get a pack of ground turkey, flat noodles, tomato sauce, and cheese.

When she grabbed the keys to Walt Diznee's new Bentley Continental, which Mr. Lopez had given him as a gift, she noticed she had one missed call.

Her heart thumped when she saw Pee Wee's number in her call log. Right away, she cleared his number and headed out the door.

M R. LOPEZ LOADED THREE HUNDRED keys into duffel bags and had them shipped to his car lot.

He didn't want to give Walt Diznee three hundred kilos of pure cocaine.

Instead, he recompressed it with cut. Four hundred grams of lactose were applied to each kilo of pure cocaine and sifted through a sieve.

Mr. Lopez felt it would be a lot safer, not only for himself but also for Walt Diznee.

He stood in his office, calculating his profits after a shipment of two thousand bricks of coke he and his two brothers in other states had received.

Mr. Lopez glanced up at the door when he heard a slight knock. "Come in!" he yelled.

"Hey, buddy, have a seat."

Walt Diznee sat down in the soft leather chair opposite Mr. Lopez. "What's up, Mr. Lopez? Is everything okay?"

"Sure, buddy, I'm fine. Well, are you ready to talk business?"

Walt Diznee smiled.

"Mr. Lopez, if I wasn't, I wouldn't be here in your office." Walt Diznee crossed his legs.

"Fair enough for me. Well, I guess I should start by saying the shipment we've been waiting on is here.

I've decided to cut my product just a bit over the percentage of being pure.

Right now, the percentage is seventy-three percent, which is very good."

Mr. Lopez reached for a Cuban cigar. After clipping the tip off, he placed the cigar into his mouth.

"I don't understand, Mr. Lopez. Why would you cut it? That's the thing: we want to have the best shit."

"Mr. Gary, listen. I'm trusting you with three hundred kilos of cocaine. It would be foolish to have you selling all that pure shit out there.

You have police that bust's their asses to catch people like us every day.

And then you got people out there on this drug, they have nothing to lose, and if they're not careful, they'll get busted with pure cocaine that is coming from us.

The only thing those pigs is wanting to know, is how in the hell they got a hold onto pure cocaine.

It's going to make them work much harder to find the source of supplier."

Walt Diznee thought about everything Mr. Lopez had told him. He agreed to the idea.

After all, three hundred bricks of cocaine was a lot.

They had to be smart, and make careful moves they were about to make. That was only half the supply; him and his team had four hundred more bricks to get rid of.

"Mr. Lopez, I've got in touch with a few people in North Carolina. I'm only allowed to supply six cities in that state.

I got Fayetteville, Wilmington, Lumberton, Durham, and Goldsboro. That's not including other states."

Mr. Lopez nodded in approval. "Okay, that's fair enough. Do you have a safe spot to house three hundred kilos?" he asked.

"Yes, I have a very close client-friend that owns houses in the Salters Cove community. It's located in Garden City, a few minutes before you reach Garden City Car Wash. We can house everything there."

"That'll be fine. Give me a few hours, and you'll be set to go."

Walt Diznee wrote down the address and handed it to Mr. Lopez. The minute he stepped out of the office, Walt Diznee received a call. When he answered the phone, he could tell something was wrong. Felicia was crying and barely could speak.

"Hello?" Walt Diznee said, but she didn't respond. "Baby, what's wrong?" She was breathing heavily into the receiver. "What's wrong, yo?" he yelled.

"Walt Diznee, I hate your sorry black ass. How in the fuck are you going to play me?"

Walt Diznee stared at his cell phone, confused. "What the fuck are you talking about?"

He was trying to gain understanding of what was going on.

"My ass went out of town for a few weeks. I came home and found that bitch in our house.

The bitch even had on the apron I bought you. And when I bought the damn thing, it said, 'Walt Diznee.'

Now it says, 'Walt Diznee Girl.'

I guess the bitch took a marker and wrote on your apron."

He couldn't believe what he was hearing. "Baby, hear me out. It's not what you're thinking, man."

She stopped him from speaking.

"You know what? I really don't have the time, Walt Diznee. Or should I say Corey? Whatever your name of choice may be, I'm fucking done playing games with your sorry ass!" she screamed.

"Felicia—"

"No, mothafucka, I ain't finished. You going to hear what the fuck I have to say.

Stupid ass nigga, I know you be on some bullshit.

I've even caught other bitches' numbers in your phone in the past.

And now you got that bitch in our house."

"Bitch, fuck you. To be honest, Felicia, I don't have time for your crying ass.

I'm trying to explain myself to you, but you don't want to fucking hear me out.

So fuck it, and fuck you, word man, i don't have time for this shit."

Before he could say anything else, Felicia hung up.

He tried calling her back, but Felicia refused to pick up.

He wanted to apologize for cussing her out. After the third call went unanswered, he gave up and decided to call his baby mother.

"Hello?" Cristal answered.

"Yo. Did anybody come by my house today?"

"Yeah, why?" She smiled.

"Some girl came by, but she didn't leave a name. She acted like she was upset when I answered the door.

She must be your little cutty buddy," she joked.

"Man, that girl is fucking crazy, yo. She think we got something going on.

I tried to explain the situation to her, but she hung up on me. So fuck it!"

He shrugged the issue out his mind.

"Well, too bad for her."

Cristal couldn't have cared less about her and what her baby daddy had going on.

"What you mean 'too bad for her'?" he asked.

"Never mind. I didn't mean nothing by that.

But guess what? Can you believe Pee Wee tried to call me earlier today? I had my phone on vibrate, so I missed the call."

He had hate and anger building up on the inside.

He didn't like the idea of Pee Wee trying to contact his baby mother. "Why in the fuck is he calling you?"

"I don't know." She sucked her teeth when she saw the traffic slow down.

"Cristal, where are you? It sounds like you're in a car."

He was still sitting in his car in Mr. Lopez's parking lot, while he spoke to her.

"I'm heading to Super Walmart. Why?"

"What the fuck is wrong with you, yo? You know Pee Wee is out to get you.

I'm on my way over there, Cristal. Whatever you do, please stay inside Super Walmart until I get there. And where is Tahshawn?"

He placed his car in drive and were heading towards the direction, to save his family's life.

"Corey, you need to stop being so paranoid. I'm a big girl, okay? And Tahshawn is right here with me. Say hi to your daddy, Tater."

"Hi, Daddy!" Tahshawn yelled from the backseat.

"Baby, listen to me," Walt Diznee begged.

"Please stay in the fucking store until I get there."

He reached under the seat for his gun and then tucked it at his waist.

He called Grasshopper and his boy Wild Child and told them to meet him at Super Walmart, just in case he was outnumbered.

I most definitely got to get rid of Pee Wee!

COREY N. SMALLS

Felicia couldn't believe she'd let her guard down for the third time in trying to find love.

The hurt and betrayal kept her up all night. She wanted to know where and how things had gone wrong.

She opened a bottle of Tylenol, poured a handful pills into her mouth, and chased them with a shot of Grey Goose.

Her head throbbed with abnormal force, she cried nonstop whenever she envisioned him with his baby mother, and their son under one roof.

Her night seemed as if it had no end.

It bothered her to know she was alone again.

That sorry bastard. I can't believe he played me.

Felicia was hurt more now than she had ever been, in her past relationships.

Only a year ago, she'd walked into her home and discovered her best friend getting fucked by her fiancé.

She had her best friend put in jail for trespassing, and charged her fiancé with assault and battery.

She'd cost him five years of his life in the federal penitentiary.

She was a firm believer in hurting the ones who hurt her.

Afterward, Felicia never thought twice about it.

She always told herself, *If the betrayer betrayed first, then it's payback! People reap what they sow.*

Felicia had trusted no man until she met Walt Diznee. She felt his pain when he talked to her about being neglected by his baby mother.

She related to his problems!

She'd given him her shoulder to lean on and her body to lust over, she couldn't turn off the love she felt for him.

She later took another shot of Grey Goose, only this time, she drank it straight from the bottle.

She pulled her Deréon heels off and threw them at the wall, and she were so hurt, she grabbed his Crown Holder button-up, and put it in the tub, with all her pictures of him

Then poured rubbing alcohol on the items, setting it all on fire.

She ran out of the restroom in search of her cell phone. Felicia dialed her employer's number and waited.

Yeah, mothafucka, you'll pay for this pain.

"You've reached the Federal Bureau of Investigation. Agent Carr speaking. How may I help you?"

"Yes, Agent Carr, this is Agent Felicia calling. I have a lead on a drug kingpin here in Myrtle Beach."

22

Pee Wee saw that Cristal was at the Super Walmart located on Seaboard Street in Myrtle Beach.

He was surprised!

She was only minutes away from his trap house. "Oh, hell nah."

He called his boys Nitty and D-Bo, who were on White Street.

He wanted Cristal out the picture. It'll help him sleep better at night, once he knew she was not around.

He couldn't get over the fact that she'd had him robbed. He wanted to teach her a valuable lesson about playing with street niggas.

"Yo, I need y'all to head to Super Walmart. That bitch is there as we speak. I pulled her up on my chaperone feature, and the map showed she's at Super Walmart, holla at me once all are said, and done."

Right away, he hung the phone up. He tried to sit still, but his adrenaline wouldn't allow him to.

The thing that bothered him the most was the loss of money.

He knew Walt Diznee were the one behind the prices being dropped.

And that drop, had slowed a lot of business down for him.

Pee Wee had been averaging $600,000 a day, but when Walt Diznee had taken the city of Myrtle Beach and the smaller towns surrounding it, Pee Wee's average had dropped to $400,000, and he only profited $100,000.

Not only did he want Cristal dead, but he wanted Walt Diznee to pay for the losses of money he'd missed over the last several months.

He didn't care about the outcome, of the situation. The nigga was desperate and refuses to lose his connect.

She'd told Pee Wee that if things didn't change for the better, he would be replaced.

Time was now running out!

Pee Wee kept pacing back and forth until he heard a knock at the door.

Before he walked toward the door, he pulled on his half blunt, but he noticed it was no longer lit.

In frustration, he tossed the half blunt onto the table, and then he answered the door.

"Cheese, what's going on?"

Pee Wee stuck his head out the door to be sure no one was following behind Cheese. When the coast was clear, he shut and locked the door behind him.

"Damn, mothafucka, you okay in this bitch?"

Cheese saw the sweat dripping down his boy's face.

He knew Pee Wee only got that way when something was about to go down.

"Cheese, I finally caught up with that bitch. I got Nitty and his brother D-Bo out there right now as we speak to out that bitch." Pee Wee was excited.

"Well, I got the scoop on the bitch too."

Pee Wee looked Cheese in the eyes, confused. "What scoop?"

"My nigga, guess who the bitch's baby daddy is?"

Pee Wee just stood there and waited for his boy to put him on the latest news update.

"Her baby daddy is Walt Diznee. So if you kill her, you have to kill Walt Diznee.

But the only problem are, if we take Walt Diznee out, we better be ready for war," Cheese said.

"So you mean to tell me he's the baby daddy she was telling me about? He was in prison, right?"

Cheese just nodded.

"Yo, Cheese, that fool is a sucker for love, man."

"To keep it real, you can call it a sucker, but I call it a crazy-ass nigga in love.

You playing, but that nigga isn't going to let anything bad happen to that bitch.

She's the mother of his child, man," Cheese said.

"Cheese, listen. I don't give a damn about that bitch, I don't give a damn about Walt Diznee, and I damn sure don't give a fuck about their son."

Cheese just shook his head.

"Well, remember that hit you put over Punch's head?" He paused.

"Yeah, what about it?"

"Punch was Walt Diznee's big cousin. The word on the streets says that he is very heated about Punch being killed.

He has a large amount of money for anybody who finds out about the hit."

Pee Wee grabbed the half blunt he'd tossed onto the table.

"You know what, Cheese? Punch had it coming to him, and he knew that.

He set Blue up with the feds a while back with five bricks. Blue was one of my main man, it was a big favor I owed him."

Pee Wee glanced at his watch and noticed it had been more than an hour since he called Nitty and D-Bo. He wanted to know what the holdup was!

He grabbed his phone and dialed Nitty's number.

Cheese just sat there staring at Pee Wee. He knew that by fucking with Walt Diznee, Pee Wee was carving his own name on a tombstone.

And although he knew that Pee Wee were on a suicidal mission, he would stand by his side no matter what.

Cheese walked to the window and stood motionless with his head toward the sky.

"Til death do us part. Amen!"

He said a small prayer and walked away:

When Walt Diznee pulled into the Super Walmart parking lot, he saw that it was busy. He drove around until he spotted a car he recognized.

He slammed on his brakes when he saw that Cristal had driven his Bentley without his permission. He was so angry that he thought about killing her himself.

Cars waiting behind him honked their horns, while he was caught up in the moment.

He pulled into a vacant spot five cars down from his Bentley and waited for Cristal and his son to come out.

As he sat there, he studied every car that came into the Super Walmart parking lot.

And the minute he saw Grasshopper, Wild Child, and his cousin Hot, he called them and told them to park by the RV in front of him.

He spotted something that caught his attention: an all-gray Can-Am Spyder RT circled the parking lot at a slow rate.

The strange looking unknown car, first got his attention because of the style, and it held his attention as it came back around for the second, third, and fourth times.

He studied the Can-Am Spyder RT and called Grasshopper.

"Yo, y'all see that all-gray Spyder RT circling the parking lot?"

Grasshopper spotted the car.

"Hell yeah, we was just talking about that shit, Why? What's on your mind?"

"Yo, they looking suspicious to me, dawg."

Walt Diznee than glanced over toward the Super Walmart entrance, to see if Cristal and his son were coming out, but he saw no one.

"Grasshopper, listen. I'm about to go in to see if I can find Cristal and my son, keep your eyes on that Spyder.

And if they even look like they're about to try anything fucked up, I want y'all to Swiss-cheese that bitch. I don't care who's around."

"Got you!" Grasshopper said.

Walt Diznee hopped out of his car and headed toward the busy entrance. He couldn't believe how many Mexicans were coming in and out of Super Walmart.

Before he reached the second automatic sliding door, he saw Cristal and his son coming out.

"Corey, what's wrong?"

He reached for his son's hand. "I think Pee Wee sent somebody here to get you."

She felt her heart pounding hard in her chest.

"Corey, what are you talking about? See, man, this is some bullshit, man."

"Baby, listen, I got niggas out here just in case something pops off, so here's what we have to do.

I'ma let you go out first!

And do not hop in the Bentley; hop in the Benz.

As a matter of fact, let me get my car keys. I have the Benz parked five slots down from the Bentley."

"So what you gonna do, Corey? You're gonna let me and Tahshawn walk out there by ourselves?" she asked.

"No, I'm going to walk behind you. I want them mothafuckas to think you are by yourself. So go straight to the fucking Benz, even if you hear a gun go off."

Everything was happening so fast. She couldn't understand why dealing with Pee Wee had turned out so violently.

"Hold up. Let me make a call."

Walt Diznee looked into her eyes and saw how bad she were afraid. He wished she would have stayed at the house, where they were safe.

But now she'd put her life, along with their son's life in danger.

"Daddy, what's going on?" Tahshawn asked.

"Son, you just do what your mother tells you. Do you hear me?" He pointed at his son.

Then he called Grasshopper.

"Yo, Cristal and my son is coming out. I need y'all to watch their front. I got the back.

I'm going to walk a few feet behind them."

He hung up the phone, gave his son a hug and kissed him on the forehead, got back up, and stared Cristal in the face.

Tears left traces on her cheeks, but he wiped them away.

"Don't cry now, because no one told your ass to leave the house when you know Pee Wee is out to get you.

As a matter of fact, you need to leave these bags of food here, yo."

He grabbed the bags and led them out the door.

"Baby, do not look back, just look ahead of you."

They began walking, and he stayed a few feet behind them.

He looked from side to side to be sure the all-gray Spyder RT wasn't approaching.

He prayed this wasn't the hit to end his son's mother's life. He felt bad that he'd put her life in danger when he had Pee Wee pistol-whipped and robbed.

He wanted to tell her that what had happened to Pee Wee that night, had been because of an order he sent out, but he refused to let her know, because she might never say anything to him again once she knew he'd put her and their son's lives on the line.

So he kept his mouth closed.

He heard a loud tire-screeching sound and the horsepower coming from a sports car after a force of acceleration.

Right away, he knew it was a hit.

He pulled out his .45 Magnum and began firing shots at the oncoming car. Grasshopper, Wild Child, and Hot jumped out of their car and started to unload the Ingram MAC-11 into the Spyder RT.

Walt Diznee ran toward Cristal and his son, trying his best to cover them, but a bullet from a .50-caliber knocked him down in between two parked cars.

He yelled for Cristal and his son to jump into the backseat and lie on the floor.

The Spyder RT rammed into other cars in the rush to get away and lost control.

Innocent bystanders got hit by stray bullets, but that didn't stop the shooters from firing back at Walt Diznee's and his men.

D-Bo tried to get out and run but caught a line of bullets across his back.

Nitty caught a few bullets in the chest.

"Yo, Walt Diznee, get the fuck out of here!" yelled Hot.

He heard Cristal and his son screaming amid the mixture of oncoming sirens. He felt where the bullet had hit him, and to his surprise, it hadn't penetrated the Teflon vest he loved to wear.

Hot and Wild Child ran over to where Walt Diznee was lying and helped him up.

"Yo, get the fuck up. You got to get out of here now," Hot said.

"Yo, where's Grasshopper?"

Walt Diznee looked around for his main shooter, who was nowhere to be found.

"He been hit. But you need to get moving."

Listening to his boy Hot, he got up and hopped into his car.

As he pulled off heading towards 501 existing Seaboard Street, he heard more shots being let off, and this time, the sound was from Hot and Wild Child's in a crossfire with the Horry County Police Department.

23

WALT DIZNEE DROPPED TAHSHAWN off at his mother's house before he and Cristal headed to where his cousin Shae Shae and Young Mafio were. It had been a week since they'd came from up north, and were already ready to head back, but they couldn't until the job was done.

Shae Shae was already a bit paranoid from the killing she'd done, on the very first night they have arrived in Myrtle Beach.

She'd stayed under the radar ever since, and kept the television on News 13 to make sure her identity hadn't been revealed.

And to her surprise, the police didn't have any information on the killer of Toya Wish.

She and Young Mafio were watching a Sub-Zero DVD when they heard a knock at the door.

Young Mafio reached for the gun he hide under a cushion of the couch he always lay on.

"Shae Shae, who's that?" he asked.

"Boy, that's my cousin. He's bringing his baby mother with him cause she knows a lot about this Pee Wee dude. You need to put that fucking gun away."

When she opened the door to let them in, she could tell right away that something bad had just happened to them. She closed the door behind them and led them down a hall and into the living room, so they could talk serious business about Pee Wee.

Cristal sat down and stared at Shae Shae as if trying to figure out where she had seen her before.

She always remembered a person's face, but for some reason, she couldn't quite put her finger on Shae Shae's last whereabouts.

"Damn, Walt Diznee, what the fuck happened to you, nigga?" Shae Shae stood over him before she sat down.

Walt Diznee glanced over at Young Mafio as if he didn't belong there.

"My bad, Walt Diznee. This is my boy Young Mafio. I brought him down with me for the extra hand on your boy. He's cool though, trust me."

Shae Shae introduced Young Mafio to her cousin and his baby mother.

"Okay, well, the time is now. I brought my baby mother to talk to you. But as for me, some bad shit took place in the Super Walmart parking lot.

That bitch ass nigga Pee Wee, somehow found out where Cristal was, and sent his boys at her and my son.

I'd just gotten back from seeing my connect, and something told me to call her ass after I got a call from Felicia. She tripping about seeing Cristal at my house."

Walt Diznee glanced over at Cristal when he mentioned Felicia, and he saw a slight blush.

"When I got to Wal Mart, I called a few people to meet me there. Then I noticed this gray Spyder RT roaming the parking lot. Right then, I knew it was a hit.

Anyway, to make a long story short, shit has gotten out of hand."

He reached for his chest, where he still felt the impact of the bullet that had hit him.

"Well, how can we find this Pee Wee, and where do he be at?"

Everyone turned to look at Cristal, as if she knew the answer to their question. It didn't take a rocket scientist to figure out her baby daddy wanted Pee Wee dead.

She couldn't believe she was about to play a part in getting him killed.

Fuck it. It's either my life or his. She thought.

"Pee Wee loves to be at this spot called Ron John's Bar and Grill off 501 Business.

He goes there only on the weekdays to pimp his bitches. To be honest with you, it's like he run that place, whatever he says goes!

But on the weekend, he's out of town to handle other business he has his hands into."

"Where is this Ron John's Bar and Grill at?" Shae Shae asked.

"It's easy to find. It's beside a firecracker store and a strip club called Tropical Beauty."

Cristal felt at ease now that she'd had the chance to release the pressure off her chest.

She wouldn't be able to breathe until she knew Pee Wee was dealt with.

"I remember that strip spot, yo. Remember that night when you went to Walt Diznee's birthday party? That's where I had you drop me off at. Yeah, and she's right; there's a bar beside that strip joint."

Young Mafio wanted to leave right away to chop Pee Wee up with his new machete, but he knew the mission had to be planned just right.

Besides, this was his girl Shae Shae's hit.

He would have to move on her demands.

Once Cristal heard what Young Mafio said about Shae Shae being at Walt Diznee's birthday party, right away, she recognized her.

Oh my, that's her.

Cristal was standing in the same room as the girl who'd saved her life.

$$C$$

"Hollywood, I'm telling you the only way to get at Walt Diznee, is through one of his brothers.

We yank one of them mothafuckas up, and hold him for ransom.

Trust me, my nigga. Walt Diznee and his big brother, Teflon, is coming off that bread."

Cheese was jealous of Walt Diznee and his brothers. He wanted to see them at the bottom.

"Cheese, that's what it is, but how are we going to get one of them niggas?" Pee Wee asked.

"That's nothing. I got their number right here."

Cheese made a call to Redeyes first, but no one answered the phone.

Cheese stood by Kendrick, and he saw Hollywood reach for his keys, as if they were about to leave.

He called Redeyes's phone for a second time but still got no answer. The next number he called was Grouch's, and Kendrick was surprised he answered his phone.

Cheese tapped Spice, who waved at Hollywood to get his attention.

Hollywood glanced at Cheese and waited.

"Grouch, what's up, my dawg? Where you at? Are you busy?" Cheese asked.

Grouch was a bit caught off guard to hear from Cheese. It had been a minute since they'd talked to each other.

But on the strength of his brother Walt Diznee, he pushed his negative thoughts about Cheese to the side.

"What's good, Cheese? I'm in North Myrtle Beach at one of my bitches' spots, Why? What's good?"

Grouch waited for Cheese to speak.

"Damn, my nigga, you're right beside me. I got this dude who's trying to cop a brick, right now and I don't have what he want on me.

I'll have to turn all the way around to get it for him. I tried to call Redeyes, but he didn't pick up."

Grouch glanced at his watch to check the time.

"Cheese, where you at right now? I'll meet you someplace."

"I'm not too far away from North Myrtle Beach Mall. You want to meet there?"

Grouch wasn't sure about meeting in a public area, but at that time of day, he felt nothing could go wrong.

"Bet it up. Meet me in front of Belk. I'll be there in ten minutes."

Cheese hung up and stared at Hollywood and smiled.

"He'll be in front of Belk in ten minutes. We need to put a move on it."

They all jumped into an all-black BMW jeep and headed toward North Myrtle Beach Mall, where they parked and waited for Grouch.

While waiting, Hollywood saw a sexy female coming out of Belk's entrance.

He called her over and began to holla. He knew they had only a few minutes before Grouch pulled up, so he moved fast.

Hollywood paid her to keep Grouch busy until he saw the coast was clear to make the hit.

They were very determined not to let Grouch get away.

Cheese spotted Grouch maneuver across the parking lot, and tapped Hollywood on the shoulder.

"Let the bitch go so she can talk to dude," he whispered.

When Grouch came to a stop, she went over to his car and knocked on the window. Once the dark tinted window came down, her heart pounded.

"Hey, Leah." Grouch was surprised to see her.

"Oh my gosh, Grouch, it's you!" Her body went numb, and her mouth became dry.

"Yeah, baby girl, it's me. What's up? You still stripping at the Bunny Ranch?"

He had lust in his eyes when he saw how thick she was.

"Fuck that, Grouch. Hurry up and pull off. Pull off now!"

Grouch could tell something wasn't right. He saw it in Leah's face and heard it in the way she yelled for him to pull off.

By the time he put his car into gear, Kendrick was already in the passenger seat with a gun held to his head.

"All right, baby boy, you know what time it is?"

Kendrick pressed the barrel of his gun against Grouch's temple.

"Look, my nigga, I got the dope in the backseat. Take it."

Grouch closed his eyes and held his hands in the air, and prayed for his life.

He couldn't believe Cheese had set him up as the lick.

Leah tried to run, but her six-inch heels slowed her down. Cheese got out of the truck and chased her.

He grabbed Leah's hair and sliced her neck from ear to ear.

Before Cheese hopped back into the BMW jeep, he stared Grouch in his eyes. Then he closed the door behind him.

"Look, man, what's this shit about?" Grouch asked.

Kendrick smiled.

"It's about business. Now, drive."

Grouch pulled off and passed Leah's lifeless body on the hot asphalt.

Cheese and Hollywood followed close behind them in case Grouch tried anything funny.

Right away, they called Pee Wee to let him know they'd gotten Grouch for ransom.

He ordered them to hide Grouch at his house, in the hideaway basement he had built in his home.

He wanted to keep Grouch hidden for a day before he completed the next part of his plan.

Yeah, Walt Diznee, it won't be fun when you hear the rabbit has the gun.

Pee Wee hopped into a stretch Hummer with seven of his bitches and headed to his favorite bar, Ron John's.

It was golf season, and golfers hung out in the bars and bowling alleys, where they would look for pretty young girls to fuck.

That night was the first night for the golfers, at starting off their vocational season, and Pee Wee was out to get his share of money his girls were soon to make.

$$\varsigma$$

Shae Shae walked into the bar, and her first impressions were of the faint weed smoke and noise. A live band was playing that night, and everyone was enjoying themselves.

She then saw a male figure surrounded with a lot of females.

He must be Pee Wee, she told herself.

She walked toward the ladies' restroom to get a better look at the opportunity to get away.

There was another exit door on the side, but it was too far away from Pee Wee's table. She'd left Young Mafio in the car to watch whatever went on outside. They both worked together very well.

She went back to the bar area, ordered a Patrón with pineapple juice, and then watched the live band.

Ten minutes later, Shae Shae noticed two more girls walk toward Pee Wee. One sat in his lap, while the other nibbled on his earlobe.

She also noticed one of the females handed him some cash. Pee Wee wrapped the bills around a larger roll he pulled from his pocket.

The unknown girl got up and left, but minutes later, another one of his bitches joined him.

Shae Shae allowed herself to have only two drinks of Patón with pineapple juice because she wanted to be careful about her shit.

She sat back and watched everyone's movements. She took note of who went where, who came, who left, and who stayed.

She observed everything about Pee Wee.

He always sat in one spot and kept his back to the wall while his bitches made their moves to make his money.

When he left for the bathroom, her timing was good; she got up and went to the ladies' restroom across from the gentlemen's restroom.

She looked around the restroom, She was alone!

She doubled back to crack the door and then peeked out and waited for him to come back out.

COREY N. SMALLS

She opened her Prada tote bag to see if her Colt automatic was off safety. Then she heard the men's restroom door open.

That's him! she thought.

She walked out and met him in the hallway. Their eyes met. He couldn't believe how sexy she was.

He had to have her, regardless of his other bitches.

"Excuse me, miss. How you doing?"

He was tipsy, and right away, she knew she had the advantage.

"I'm doing fine." She blushed as if she were shy, as planned, and knew it would go well.

Shae Shae walked off, and he followed behind to get a better look at her ass.

He grabbed his dick and squeezed it, as if he couldn't control his desire to feel his dick in her soft pussy.

She looked over her shoulder, giving him a flirtatious smile without any serious intent. She knew she had to show casual interest to bring Pee Wee closer to her kill.

"What's your name, miss?"

He tried to talk over the loud music.

"You can call me Obsession, boo boo." She gave an alias, as usual. She never gave strangers her name.

In fact, she gave every man she met an alias, which made it more difficult for anyone to find her.

"What is it, you're obsessed about?"

Shae Shae stared him in the eyes. "Bad boys."

He laughed.

"What type of bad boys? I mean, there's so many." He smiled.

"The type of bad boys I'm obsessed over are killers and drug dealers.

It seems to me you don't fit the description, honey."

She took another sip of her drink, bobbing her head to the music the live band played.

"Don't judge a book by its cover, baby. I know you've heard that before."

She smiled and looked at the group of girls waiting on Pee Wee to return.

"Well, the truth is, I'm not judging a book by its cover. I'm calling things how I see it."

She stuck her tongue out at him in a way that drove him crazy.

"So what do you see?" Pee Wee asked while looking around the bar.

"I see a squirrel with a long, bushy tail, that's trying to get a nut." She pointed at the group of girls looking in their direction.

"Oh no, no, please don't let the bitches fool you. I'm their daddy! You know, p-i-m-p.

My squirrel days are long gone. I'm the man around here," he boasted proudly.

"You know what? I've always wanted me a daddy. It's just that I can't find the right one to pamper me."

Pee Wee took a sip from his cup of Crown Royal on the rocks. She'd told him just what he wanted to hear.

She wanted a daddy. She wanted to be pimped out. Pee Wee felt he could use a fresh piece of pussy on his team.

He would turn her out by giving her all the things she wanted, and then later, she'll cater to him.

Yeah, bitch, as pretty as you are, you'll be my main money ho.

"Well, baby, I can be your daddy. Are you up for adoption?"

Shae Shae liked the pickup line; she had to give him that. He was a good talker.

"So you think you can make me happy?" she asked.

"Obsession, check this out: I'm the mothafucking messiah without the twelve disciples. I'll make anything happen for you, baby."

He shot the last of his Crown Royal down in one gulp.

"Nigga, please. You ain't that damn powerful." She laughed at him flirtatiously.

"Baby, hear me out. I know we just met, but I want to take you home. I need to get my mouth wet.

We don't have to fuck; just let me taste your pussy.

Remember, you've told me you're obsessed with killers and drug dealers.

Well, if you come home with me tonight, I'll give you pure excitement of a killer."

He stared deep into her eyes without blinking.

"I'll take you up on that offer. I mean hell, it's been a minute since I had the seeds picked out of my watermelon.

By the way, what's your name?"

She wanted to be sure she had the right man.

"It's Pee Wee."

"No, nigga, it's Dead Man. 'Cause I'ma kill your ass."

CHAPTER 24

WALT DIZNEE AND HIS WORKERS were boxing the last load of dope to be shipped to the five cities of North Carolina. His first business with Lumbee and Cherokee Indians had made him millions of dollars.

He paused at the vision that flashed before him.

Déjà vu! He whispered.

He looked around and saw Redeyes at the money counter next to three round tables piled with stacks of money.

He couldn't believe what was going on around him.

He later walked over to Jennifer after she got off the phone with Mr. Lopez.

She smiled when she saw him approaching her. She put her arms around his waist and kissed him on the mouth.

"Veni, vidi, vici," he said.

She sucked her teeth. "Stop being so big-headed, boy."

She pinched him on the hip.

"What? You don't think I know Latin?"

Walt Diznee laughed. "Okay, Miss Know-It-All. What did I say?"

"You said, 'I came, I saw, I conquered.'" She repeated his comment in English.

"Honey, listen. I know four different languages: Latin, French, English, and my own, which is Spanish.

Now let me see where your head is at.

So if I say, 'Audentes fortuna juvat,' what does that mean?" She held him so close they could have kissed.

"Baby, that means 'Fortune favors the bold.'"

"Boo, you're right about that, though." She grabbed his dick and then looked around to see if anyone saw them.

"Can I have it a tergo?" she whispered.

"So you want it from behind?" Walt Diznee looked her in the eyes.

"Lusus naturae, baby girl."

She squeezed his dick harder. "Of course. I'm a freak of nature. Bien entendu. That means 'Well understood.'"

They walked into the next room to get a quickie, when Walt Diznee received a call from Cheese.

He wanted to hand Redeyes the phone because he really wanted to fuck at the moment, but when he glanced over and saw his brother busy counting money, he decided to just let the phone ring.

Jennifer slammed the door behind them and pulled Walt Diznee's pants past his knees. She put his dick in her mouth, grabbed his long balls, and massaged them while sucking on his mushroom-shaped head.

She was in love with the taste of his dick. She began to jack him off, looking him in his weak eyes.

She knew it felt good to him, and it made her pussy wet when he pulled her hair.

His cell phone beeped just before he was about to bust his nut. He reached for his phone and noticed Cristal had sent him a text message.

"Damn!" he whispered to himself.

She wanted to see him because she missed him so much. Even though she was staying at his home, she couldn't get enough of Walt Diznee. After giving him the pussy, she was hooked.

He grabbed Jennifer by the arm and pulled her up. "Come here, baby. Turn around, and show me that pussy."

She pulled her pants down and slide her thong to the side, letting him eased his way inside her wet pussy.

Every time he went deep into her, she would force herself backward, grinding her hips into his pelvic area.

He spanked her on the ass and then grabbed her waist, pulling himself deeper and faster into her with every hard thrust.

Right before he busted his nut, he leaned forward to bite her neck to keep from moaning out loud. She felt his dick swell inside her tight pussy.

Right away, she used the muscles of her juicy walls and squeezed as hard as she could, to drain him of every nut that existed in his body.

Walt Diznee couldn't help but call her name. The feeling of her gripping his dick with her pussy felt so damn good.

They both laughed as they collapsed onto the floor.

"Damn, baby, where'd you learn to grip a dick like that? You blew my fucking mind with that one," he teased.

"Nigga, you know my pussy is the bomb."

He smiled while breathing heavily. "Real talk. That pussy is good, boo boo."

She pulled his soft dick out of her. It was wet and glossy from her cum. She stuck his dick back into her mouth and sucked him dry.

After she licked the last of her cum off him, she lightly nibbled on the tip of his soft dick head.

"Forsan et haec olim meminisse juvabit."

Walt Diznee stared at her as if he were lost. "Boo, you got me on that one. What that meant?" he asked while trembling.

"I said, 'Perhaps this too will be a pleasure to look back on one day.'" She smiled.

"Oh, most definitely. But right now, let's make sure this load of dope gets to where it needs to be. And I need to find out where in the fuck Grouch is at."

Walt Diznee tried calling his phone, but it went straight to voice mail.

Pee Wee wanted Grouch to die slowly, so he called one of his ex-whores he used to pimp before she got infected with full-blown AIDS.

Kay Kay had made Pee Wee lots of money in her time. She was Filipino but had grown up in California.

She'd come to Myrtle Beach a few years ago for Black Bikers Week where she'd fallen in love with the environment, and never returned home.

She had met up with Pee Wee and later had become accustomed to his pimp service. She always had came with his money and never tried to play him in any way, form, or fashion.

She had always been loyal to Pee Wee. And whenever he'd needed a bitch beat down, she always had been up for the job.

Not only was she pretty, but she had the heart of a lion as well.

However, when she'd gotten infected, Pee Wee had let her go. But he always kept her close to him.

He never knew when she could be of great use.

And that night was the first time he'd called her in two months, and that was from the last lick she'd helped him on.

When Kay Kay walked into the room, she saw Grouch sitting in a chair with a pillowcase over his head, with chains at his feet and arms. "Hey, babe, are you okay?" she said to him as she walked towards him.

Grouch tried to move when he felt her unzip his pants and pull his dick out.

"It's okay, boo. I'm not here to hurt you. Have you ever fucked a girl with full-blown AIDS before? You should try it babe. It's as good as any other pussy you've fucked in the past."

She was crazy, sure as shit.

Grouch tried his best to yell, but the duct tape around his mouth muffled his voice. He rocked back and forth from side to side, causing the chair to tilt over and knocking himself to the floor.

Kay Kay set the chair back up and started to suck his dick to get him hard.

Grouch tried his best not to think about the feeling being so good. He knew she was setting him up for the kill.

She knew Grouch couldn't resist how well she sucked his dick. He began to grow hard. Kay Kay slid his dick down her throat, making him harder.

"Yeah, babe, let me see this pretty dick grow."

She started to jack him off while sliding her tongue through the slit of his pee hole. She felt him squeezing his dick muscle to the feeling. Then she climbed on top of him cowgirl style.

As she put him inside her, Grouch began to head-butt her. She got mad and slapped him in the face.

Kay Kay pushed his head backward and held it in place as she straddled him.

She moved faster when she began to cum. "Mmm." Kay Kay moaned.

She fucked him harder to make him cum.

"Welcome to my world, baby."

She got off him and then put his dick back in his pants.

Before she left, Kay Kay pulled the pillowcase just above his mouth to kiss his lips through the duct tape.

"Maybe we could do this again sometime." She turned around to leave the room and met Kendrick, Cheese, and Hollywood at the door.

They handed her a bag of money before walking into the room.

Kendrick pulled her by the arm. "Kay Kay, listen. You don't know anything. You hear me?" He spoke aggressively.

"Boy, don't come at me with some bullshit like that. You know I'm not new to this shit, nigga.

Besides, I'm working for Pee Wee, not you." She yanked her arm away, leaving him standing there.

Damn, I can't stand that bitch.

Kendrick walked into the room and closed the door behind him. He pulled the pillowcase from Grouch's head and tossed it into his lap.

Grouch stared at Cheese as if he were the only one there with him. He wanted to kill Cheese so badly that tears came running down his cheeks.

Cheese tried to look Grouch in the eyes, but his guilt kept his eyes wandering in other places.

Kendrick grabbed a baseball bat and started to beat Grouch in the legs.

The first swing cracked his knee. The pain made him faint, but when Hollywood punched him in the face, the blow woke him back up.

Grouch couldn't believe he was going through this torture. He wanted to know the cause of it all.

They kept beating him in the ribs, knocking the breath out of him.

Cheese wanted to stop them from beating Grouch so badly, but it was far too late. They all took turns beating him over and over for the next hour.

Cheese thought he was dead but found Grouch still breathing. "Aight, pussy boy, you want to let us know where your big brother keep that bread?"

Grouch tried to look at Hollywood through his swollen eyes, but he couldn't see.

He was too exhausted and weak to hold his head up.

Hollywood motioned for Cheese to pull the duct tape from Grouch's mouth.

Grouch smiled with his head leaning back, showing them through his missing teeth and blood that, regardless of how badly they beat him, he would never roll on his brothers.

He used the last bit of strength he had to pull his head up. Then he spit blood into Cheese face.

"Death before dishonor, bitch-ass nigga."

Before Cheese had the chance to grab the baseball bat from Kendrick, Pee Wee and Shae Shae walked through the door.

"Cheese, that's enough!" Pee Wee yelled.

CHAPTER 25

Later that night, Walt Diznee and Cristal were heading to Rioz Brazilian Steakhouse, when he received a phone call from Pee Wee.

Pee Wee had his brother Grouch and wanted a million dollars.

If Walt Diznee called the police or didn't give him the money, he would kill his brother.

"Walt Diznee, when this phone hangs up, I'll be sending you something."

Pee Wee remained quiet for a moment before adding,

"There's something I really want you to see. Just to show you how serious I am. So don't do anything funny mothafucka."

Walt Diznee heard his being tortured by one of Pee Wee's men in the background.

He shook from the anger he held within. "Pee Wee, I swear on your mother and mines, that if anything happens to my brother, I will kill you slowly."

Walt Dizne threatens Pee Wee.

"Hold up, big-time. If you threaten me one more damn time, I'll swing this fucking baseball bat at your brother's head like I'm trying to win the World Series. Do you hear me?"

Before Walt Diznee could respond, he heard his little brother on the other end.

"They're going to kill me, Walt. They already fucked me up pretty bad, yo. They said if you don't come up with the money, they're going to cut me up."

The phone was shut off.

Seconds later, Walt Diznee tried calling Shae Shae.

"Baby, what's wrong? Are you okay?" Cristal was concerned about what was going on.

"Hell nah, they got my fucking brother."

Walt Diznee punched the dashboard of his baby mother's new BMW jeep.

"Who does?" she asked confusedly.

"Who does, Corey? The cops?"

Still, he didn't respond.

Her heart pounded with fear when Walt Diznee sat in the passenger seat in a daze.

"Oh my God, Corey, what's going on? And which brother do they have?"

Without saying another word, he showed his baby mother a picture from Pee Wee's text.

She screamed with fear, losing control of the X5 jeep.

Walt Diznee quickly reached for the steering wheel to regain control of the jeep before they wrecked.

"What the fuck? What is wrong with you?" he yelled.

"I need you to stay focused, Cristal."

Her body shook uncontrollably. She was too horrified to drive.

"Baby, pull over. I'll take it from here," he said.

"Oh my God. Oh my God." She was having a panic attack.

"Just pull the fuck over!" He yelled.

He spoke with frustration and anger, without speaking another word, she pulled to the side of the highway so they could swap seats.

"Baby, I got to call Teflon. We need to get our brother back. We have to keep this shit as quiet as possible.

If Mama and Daddy hear about this shit, they're going to have a fucking breakdown. First Punch got killed, and now this bullshit."

Moments later, he received a second call with a reduced offer.

The ransom was now at $500,000. The caller's voice made Walt Diznee pause.

He knew the second call was not from Pee Wee, although it had come from Pee Wee's number.

The caller sounded a bit more nervous.

He couldn't believe it was him.

Cheese? he thought.

They had less than twenty-four hours. The caller wanted the ransom money to be dropped off at an open-view area so they could watch who came and left.

He tried calling Teflon, but Teflon had flown to Zululand.

Ever since his brother had purchased his new private jet, Teflon barely stayed in the country.

Walt Diznee and Cristal drove to the Legacy apartment complex, where he rented an apartment to house his money.

After they parked, before they got out, they noticed a helicopter fly right above their heads.

"It seems like them mothafuckas is following us Cristal. I noticed that same helicopter before we left Myrtle Beach." He felt as if he were losing his mind.

"What makes you think that helicopter is following you?

You need to worry about getting your brother back. And why are we here anyway?" she looked around the complex as if she were lost.

The apartment was beautiful, as if a designer had done the interior and furnishings.

She then noticed photos of two boys who looked just like Walt Diznee.

She walked over to the two photos, which sat on the coffee table, and studied them.

She noticed their son and another unknown image. The two looked as if they were twins—same complexion, eyes, nose, and smile.

Oh God. Is that his son?

She couldn't believe it. The relation showed on the image's face.

She felt her world caved in from top to bottom, when she spotted an open case of Magnum condoms.

When she heard the sound of a loud machine, she hurried and pulled the remaining condoms out to count them.

Five were missing from the pack!

She wanted to be sure whether or not this was his home away from home, she ran to the refrigerator to see if there was any pork or red meat stored inside.

Her knees trembled when she saw nothing but vegetables, chicken, and turkey products.

She walked towards the bedroom, where she saw him closing the large steel door to his safe. She couldn't believe the amount of money he had stashed away.

"Cristal, come help me load this money into these duffel bags. Come on, baby!

We got to get going," He was rushing.

"I'll help, but let me ask you something."

She tossed the open pack of condoms onto the bed next to him, and he stared it.

"I guess whoever stayed here has a big dick like yours." She felt a sense of jealousy coming on.

"Those are mine. You know how old them shit is? That's before we even got back together."

He hated explaining himself to people.

"So this is your apartment?" Cristal asked.

"It's mine, but I have it in my little cousin Toya's name. She lives in Baltimore. I lived here before I bought my house.

I just kept this apartment for my money. No one knows about this spot but my brothers. And now you."

He was still counting money and stuffing the duffel bags. He tossed one bag across his shoulder, knocking a Bible onto the floor, and walked out of the room.

Cristal reached over to pick the old Bible up, and left it open on the nightstand next to the king-size bed.

She thought about their future and what it would be like with their second child.

I wonder. Should I tell him about me being pregnant?

"No, I think I should wait until the time is right," she whispered.

When he came back for the last bag of money, she just sat there looking at him.

She could tell he had a lot on his mind.

Seeing him stressing about his little brother made her want to cry, but she had to remain strong for her baby daddy.

"Baby, when you left with the first bag of money, you knocked your Bible onto the floor. I put it on the nightstand for you.

I didn't know what chapter you had it on, so I just left it on this page."

Ecclesiastes chapter 2 came back to haunt him—the message he'd heard in his dream, the one his grandmother had spoken.

He picked the Bible up to read:

Yet when I surveyed all that my hands had done, and what I had toiled to achieve, everything was meaningless, a chasing after the wind.

"Holy shit!"

He were very shocked.

Walt Diznee left his baby mother back at his old apartment and headed toward the Myrtle Beach Convention Center, where Pee Wee wanted the bag of money dropped off.

He sat and waited until he got the next order.

For the first time, he understood what his grandmother had been trying to tell him.

He replayed the dream in his head and then the scripture he'd read from the book of Ecclesiastes.

Damn, is that what she was trying to tell me? This life I'm living is meaningless?

He thought about the death of his cousin Punch, wondering if he'd been the cause of it.

He thought of the danger he'd brought toward his baby mother and son, because of his jealous ways.

He'd abused his power in the drug game, and now it was costing him money.

The ones closest to him were losing their lives to the streets. And now he was giving away half his street wealth to save his little brother's life.

Everything he had achieved was meaningless—a chasing after the wind.

All he wanted now, was his little brother Grouch back.

He wiped tears away.

Fuck this street life. All this shit isn't worth it. I need to get my shit together. I have what I wanted the most: my son and the love of my life.

He felt more tears running down his face.

Once I get my brother back, I'm giving all this street shit up. For good!

He looked up and noticed two black Suburbans, four all-black Crown Vics, and nine black Hummers, all windows tinted pitch black, heading in his direction at top speed.

He saw the helicopter that had followed them flying right above him.

"What the fuck?" Walt Diznee yelled.

He sped off, trying to get away, hitting parked cars, trying his best not to get caught.

Myrtle Beach police and state troopers, along with federal officials, were now behind him. He dodged in and out of traffic, putting up a fight to get away, but the helicopter clocked his every move.

He stomped down hard on the accelerator of the BMW X5. He was already at 145 miles per hour, fighting for more speed.

He kept looking back and By the minute, more cops popped up.

He thought about Cristal and his son, Tahshawn.

Damn, I just got my fucking family back.

What bothered him most was the thought of going back to prison.

He was in a high-speed chase with $500,000 in the backseat.

He couldn't get caught, he didn't want to be caught.

Walt Diznee thought about all the bullshit he'd gone through to get his family back. The more he thought about Cristal and their son, the harder he fought to get away.

She didn't even know that her baby daddy was being chased by federal authorities in the streets.

He thought about what would happen to his brother if he got caught.

Would Pee Wee kill him?

Walt Diznee felt he wouldn't be able to live with himself if anything bad happened to his brother.

"Fuck!" He cussed himself when he saw busy traffic ahead.

Any chance of getting away was out of the picture now.

He came to a halt and looked around as if that day were the last time he'd see daylight.

Everything around him seemed to move in slow motion.

His cell phone rang, and he looked down and saw that it was his son's mother.

He didn't want to answer.

He didn't want to tell her that county and federal authorities were surrounding him.

Instead, he destroyed his phone by dipping it into the cup of coffee Cristal had left in her jeep.

The FBI pointed AR15s and M16 assault rifles at the jeep. "Come out with your hands in the air!"

He was angry with himself!

When he stepped out of the jeep, he couldn't believe his eyes.

She stood only a few feet away from him.

They stared at each other while he was being handcuffed.

She walked up to him and read him his Miranda rights.

"You have the right to remain silent. Anything you say can and will be used against you in a court of law.

You have the right to talk to an attorney and have him or her present with you while you are being questioned. If you cannot afford to hire an attorney, one will be appointed to represent you before any questioning if you wish.

You can decide at any time to exercise these rights and not answer any questions or make any statements."

Without speaking another word, Detective Felicia turned and walked away.

WALT DIZNEE WAS HELD IN SOLITARY confinement at a federal detention center in Effingham, Florence County. And his phone use was restricted.

He wasn't allowed to have outside contact to anyone.

He knew it wasn't much they could charge him with, other than tax evasion and money laundering.

He kept telling himself it was just like the movies.

They'll put you in a small box where it's cold and give you little food to eat while they stand behind mirrored glass, watching you, just hoping to find ways to make a nigga talk.

The feds' way of building indictments on people, is other people to talk on others. But he wanted to see Felicia and prayed she could tell him what was going on.

That bitch isn't gonna help me. I just left her ass for my baby mama. Damn, I fucked up.

He felt bad about what had taken place only a few hours ago between him and Felicia, and the episode that had taken place at his home.

Damn, I fucked up bad, man.

Walt Diznee stared at the mirror-tinted window. He knew Felicia was there staring at him—probably laughing at him.

He remembered when she'd told him she saved Teflon from federal indictments.

And the only thing that ran through his mind, was how could she help him. He'd gotten caught red-handed with $500,000—straight blood and drug money he made while selling drugs.

Before he'd been transferred to federal holding in Effingham, he'd spent three days at J. Reuben Long Detention Center in Horry County.

He was running out of patience! And he needed to talk to someone on the outside. His brother Grouch's life was in danger.

Man, what the fuck is Shae Shae doing out there? Pee Wee should've been hit by now.

He wanted Pee Wee dead.

Walt Diznee prayed that none of his money was marked.

If that money comes back clean, I'm going to tell them my granddaddy left me that shit when he passed away.

He had his story in line.

Hell yeah. That's my story. When my granddaddy was alive, he never kept money in the bank. He always controlled his own money. It's a traditional belief that's been in my family for years.

He stared into the mirror-tinted glass and smiled.

He got up to pace the small room and heard the door open. Seconds later, a female agent came into the cell with him.

She sat opposite him at the small table, opened a manila envelope, and pulled out four large photos.

She slid them toward him.

"Do you know any of these guys?" she asked.

"Look, I have the right to remain silent. I also have the right to contact my attorney. Aren't those my rights?

Y'all have kept me fucking hostage for four days. I have the right to call my lawyer."

His eyes were bloodshot. He didn't blink.

"No one let you contact your attorney, sir?" Detective Carr asked.

"Man, do not come at me with that bullshit. You know I didn't call my fucking lawyer."

Walt Diznee stared at her, making her feel uncomfortable.

"Okay, I'll let you contact your attorney, but I need you to tell me why you were sitting in the Myrtle Beach Convention Center parking lot, with five hundred thousand dollars in your car." She waited for him to answer.

"I need to call my lawyer. What the fuck? I don't even know who you are."

"I'm sorry, sir, but my name is Detective Carr, and I'm assigned to investigate your case. Now, if you'll help me, we can help you.

At the moment, you are being charged with tax evasion and money laundering, which carry a zero to five years prison sentence.

But with you, I'm seeing that you're a career criminal. Your past record will push your prison sentence anywhere from ten to life.

So if you don't talk now, you're going to be in prison for a long time."

Walt Diznee looked the detective in the eyes.

"Like I stated earlier, I need to speak with my lawyer."

Detective Carr was becoming aggravated. She knew Walt Diznee wasn't going to cooperate with her.

"Okay. I see you want to do things the hard way. I'm going to let you make a call. One call only."

She then left the interrogation room, leaving him alone.

She went back behind the mirror-tinted window where another detective stood, and watched him.

Detective Carr looked over at her girl Felicia, who was standing there staring at the man she'd fallen in love with. He was now in her custody.

"He wants to contact his attorney. He's not talking, girl."

Felicia wanted to see him sent to prison for a long time. She didn't want him free for his baby mother to have him.

"I want that nigga to suffer long and hard, yo. That nigga really did hurt my feelings."

Felicia would try everything in her power to see him go down.

She told her superior that he was a kingpin, but she didn't have any proof. All they had on him was money.

They ran his name, hoping whatever he had would be seized and put under investigation, but to their surprise, they could only seize one car.

She knew about the two-thousand-square-foot home, the Bentley, and the kilos of cocaine he pushed into the streets.

She wanted to bring him down without Teflon having any suspicions about her involvement.

"Detective Carr, is there any chance we can have the money that was seized, tested for any trace of drugs?

If there's any trace of drugs on that money, we could bring forth indictments for conspiracy."

Felicia was brainstorming the types of charges she could hit him with.

"Look, even if there are traces of drugs on that money, we cannot indict him on conspiracy. That's impossible."

Detective Carr sucked her teeth at Felicia. Felicia was being childish in the way she was acting, and it was beginning to make her upset.

"Detective Carr, all we have to do is find a cause on that money being drug money. Then we can get any of these fools to give statements saying they've dealt with Walt Diznee a few times in the past.

Once we get them to do that, we can bring him down for conspiracy."

Detective Carr stood still, looking her in the face.

"Girl, you are fucking tripping, don't let your emotional feelings override your intelligence.

I understand he hurt you!

But you have to play cool, and if they find out we are getting people to lie about their dealings with Walt Diznee, we're going down!

I mean, you are my girl and all, but I'm not losing my job behind your ass.

Let's deal with what we have!

He's going to do prison time. You can best believe that."

"Mr. Martin, before we talk about anything dealing with me, I need you to call my brother. This is some real important shit."

Walt Diznee's mouth went dry. He needed to get to his brother Grouch, who were in danger.

"Mr. Gary, what do you need me to do?"

Walt Diznee looked him in the eyes.

"Look, you know I trust you. And we've been dealing with each other for some time now.

I'm pretty sure if Mr. Lopez trusts you, I should as well." He paused.

"I'm here for you, sir. I want you to be sure of that. Now, what do you need me to do?"

Walt Diznee had no choice but to trust his attorney if he wanted to save his brother's life.

"That day when I got caught with that half a mill, that money was to pay a ransom."

The thought of his brother being beaten by Pee Wee almost made him snap.

"Hold on, sir. Did you say *ransom*? Who got kidnapped?"

The hurt was visible in Walt Diznee's eyes. He hoped his brother was still alive.

"My little brother! And the person you'll be calling is Redeyes. Tell him Pee Wee got Grouch, and he's demanding five hundred thousand dollars to get him back.

Mr. Martin, be sure no one knows about me being picked up by the feds. If the word gets out, my little brother will lose his life. That's if he's not already dead."

Mr. Martin wrote the information down quickly.

"Mr. Gary, is there anything else you need me to do?"

He wanted to be sure he had everything he needed to do for his client.

"Yes, there's one more person you need to contact for me, my baby mother. Her name is Cristal. Let her know what's going on."

He felt sick at the thought of her leaving him again.

The thought of her being with someone else destroyed him.

"Okay, Mr. Gary, I'm on it. I'll be back real soon to let you know the outcome of it all.

Just do yourself a favor, and don't say a word to anyone. You hear me? Not a soul.

In three months, I'll have you going in front of a judge to have a bond set. I don't see where there's a problem to have you out on bond. After all, it's only money they got off you."

Mr. Martin stood up and closed his briefcase.

"Mr. Martin, are you sure about that? 'Cause these mothafuckas have me labeled as a kingpin. All they have on me is money?"

He was stressing about the charges the feds has against him.

"Let's not worry about that. Besides, no drugs were confiscated, okay?

Well, let me go take care of this situation with your brother, and I'll be back to speak with you, concerning your proffer agreement."

Walt Diznee shook his head. He was stressing about his brother, Cristal, and his son.

"What the hell is a proffer agreement?" He was confused by the legal vocabulary and wanted his lawyer to be a bit more specific.

"Mr. Gary, didn't you told me that these people are labeling you a kingpin?"

Walt Diznee nodded.

"Well, we need to do a proffer agreement to stop any superseding indictments.

Meaning if there are others giving statements on their involvement with you, their statements won't hold, and they won't be able to indict you for conspiracy.

But there is a catch. In order to do the proffer agreement, you'll have to basically tell them where all that money came from.

In so many words, you'll have to tell on yourself to save yourself."

After Mr. Martin left the interview room, Walt Diznee was moved into population.

He couldn't understand how he could save himself by telling on himself.

However, It didn't sound right. He'd always felt that only fools would hang themselves.

Regardless of the situation, h e had his own belief. It'd be best to tell his lawyer a lie.

No lawyer could be trusted!

It didn't matter how much you paid, or how much a lawyer showed interest in fighting for you and defending you.

Lawyers could only fight based on what they were told, whether it was the truth or a lie.

Walt Diznee would tell lies—all lies.

I'd be a fucking fool to tell them I sell drugs to get that money.

He began to search for familiar faces, hoping he didn't see anyone he'd dealt with.

"Hell yeah, I'm good. I never dealt with any of these mothafuckas," he whispered.

Before he sat down, he saw Napo walking out of his cell.

"What the fuck?"

His heart began to pound.

His mouth went dry. He walked to the phone, picked up the receiver, and turned his back in the opposite direction, hoping Napo didn't see him.

Damn, Napo got picked up by the feds? he thought surprisingly.

He thought back to the last time he'd dealt with Napo, and by his calculation, it had been almost six months ago.

When he turned around, Napo was standing right behind him waiting to use the phone.

"Oh shit, Walt Diznee. What the fuck happened yo?

Man, don't tell me the feds got you." Napo seemed excited to see someone he knew.

"Hell yeah, they caught me with a gun. 'Cause you remember I was in prison almost a year ago. And then my dumb ass had to sign that gun-act bullshit."

He didn't want to let Napo know about his real charges, so he gave him false information. "Napo, what they got you for, my dawg?"

"Walt Diznee, these mothafuckas got me with intent to purchase five kilos of cocaine."

Napo dropped his head.

To most niggas, when someone dropped thier head, it was a sign of weakness.

"How in the fuck did you get intent to purchase five kilos of cocaine?" Walt Diznee stared at Napo in a strange way.

"The dude I was buying it from was with the feds—that's how."

Walt Diznee couldn't believe what he was hearing.

"Napo, where did that shit happen?"

"That shit happened in North Myrtle Beach, right off Cherry Grove."

Napo explained little about his situation. "What's the deal with Redeyes and Grouch?"

None of your business, nigga.

Off the jump, Walt Diznee didn't trust him.

"Damn, my nigga, you haven't heard. My little brothers got killed in a real bad car wreck coming from Atlanta a few months ago."

Napo looked away as if the horrible news crushed his heart.

"Napo, let me go and lay it down, man. I'm tired as hell.

Talk to you later, my dawg."

Walt Diznee wanted to get away from him because he didn't want to be questioned about anyone else in his crew.

Every time Napo came by his cell, he would tell him he was reading a book, or writing a letter to Cristal.

"Eh, what kind of book are you reading?" Napo asked during one visit.

Walt Diznee glanced up at the door to face him and held the book up.

"I'm reading *The Coldest Winter Ever*. I'll holla at you later, yo."

Napo left.

Walt Diznee told him anything to keep Napo moving. He felt after a while, he'd get the picture.

Printed in the United States
By Bookmasters